Lynch Law

McLain spun sideways as a gaping hole was blasted around the lock. He kicked the door, hurling through as it swung open. Sloane was down on the floor screaming in raw terror as he struggled to push the dead man from him. Ben was behind the bar, thumbing paper cartridges into the scattergun. He snapped the breech closed as McLain came through. Bottles exploded, sending splinters of glass and streamers of whiskey across the room. McLain went down in a long dive, triggering the Dragoon. His shot splintered wood from the front of the bar. Then Ben was on his feet and running . . .

Available in Fontana by the same author

HAWK 1: THE SUDDEN GUNS
HAWK 2: BLOOD MONEY
HAWK 3: DEATH'S BOUNTY
HAWK 4: KILLING TIME
HAWK 5: FOOL'S GOLD
HAWK 6: BLOOD KIN
HAWK 7: THE GATES OF DEATH
HAWK 8: DESPERADOES
HAWK 9: THE WIDOWMAKER
HAWK 10: DEAD MAN'S HAND

PEACEMAKER 1: COMMANCHE!
PEACEMAKER 2: OUTLAWS
PEACEMAKER 3: WHIPLASH

William S. Brady

Lynch Law

Fontana/Collins

First published by Fontana Books 1981

Made and printed in Great Britain by
William Collins Sons & Co. Ltd, Glasgow

For a man with the edge:
Terry Harknett

Prologue

The place had grown.

Once it was just a wide river valley: sheltered by the surrounding hills, lush with grass. Buffalo had grazed there and the Comanche – the Nokoni and the Penatekas – had hunted the great herds. The Spanish had come, then the Americans. They had fought, and the men from the North had claimed the land. The War Between the States had stripped the valley of men and the Comanche had come again into their own. But the war ended and the men returned, blue clad, battle-hardened, to take back the land. A garrison was established and with the coming of the military there came also settlers. A few at first, braver – or more foolhardy – than most, coming to build a new life in a new place. Followed by others so that where once there were only the earthworks and the fortified shacks of the Army there was now a settlement.

Outside the place, where the trail came in from San Antonio, there was a sign. It was tall enough to hang a man from, and the board was etched with the single word, the name of the town: Garrison. Beyond the sign there was a watchtower, fifteen feet high, overlooking the earthworks and wooden walls that surrounded the place. There was a command post and a barracks large enough to house the forty soldiers stationed there. There was a saloon and a store, a blacksmith's and a livery stable, a barber shop that was also a funeral parlour, a scattering of cabins. On the perimeter, where the fortifications curved towards the river, there were tents with whores from Mexico.

It was a town, and it was called Garrison.

*

The man had grown, too.

He had come to Texas looking for a new life, with nothing to his name but a brace of Colt's Dragoon pistols, a Sharps .50 buffalo gun, and the maroon shirt of a Missouri guerrilla. He had lost everything else – wife, farm, friends. In the valley he had found new friends and a new place to build a life. He had become part of the settlement. He was a scout and a teamster; a bouncer on occasion; and the people of Garrison had come to look on him as one of them. He was the nearest thing they had to a Peace Officer.

His name was John T. McLain.

Chapter One

Mary Koch was wearing a blue dress the day she died.

It was her favourite dress, the colour matching the cornflower shade of her eyes, complementing her sun-golden hair. It had little white flowers picked out round the cuffs of the sleeves and around the hem. It was Mary's best dress, worn only on special occasions. Like a barn raising or a visit to Garrison. Mary had only two dresses – her family was not rich, and what money they made from the cattle they ran with the French Seven herds got ploughed back into the land. The sod cabin they had built when they came to the Rio Verde valley was already expanded beyond its original single room, so that now there were three separate rooms and a porch out front overlooking the tiny garden where Mary struggled to grow flowers. They had their brand on nearly two hundred head; the spring round-up would top that number.

Mary was a pretty girl. Especially so on that hot spring day because her face was alive with anticipation of the coming trip to town. There was a troupe of travelling actors passing through, and they had agreed to put on a performance. Everyone was going. And everyone would be dressed in their best: so Mary had donned her blue dress and brushed her hair until it shone. She had put on her one pair of good shoes. Shiny, high-button shoes from Abraham Kintyre's store, that the trader said had come all the way from St Louis. She had fastened a necklace of little silver links about her throat, a necklace that had belonged to her grandmother back in Germany. She felt that she could hold her own when she went to town.

Mary Koch was twelve years old.

*

'You think it's all right?'

Alice Docherty fussed with the neckline of her dress, smoothing it over the stiffness of her corset. Behind her, face reflected in the full-length mirror, Janey Page smiled and nodded.

'Alice, you look wonderful. You'll be the prettiest woman there.'

Alice smiled back. It wasn't true and she knew it. It couldn't be true, not with her close on sixty, her hair grey and her face showing too many lines. Not with someone like Janey to afford a comparison. Someone with hair the shade of ripening wheat and a figure that didn't need a set of stays to firm the breasts or flatten the stomach. But it was nice of the younger woman to say it.

'It's not too . . .' She paused, eyeing the neckline. 'Well . . .'

'No.' Janey laughed: a musical sound. 'It's not too anything. It's perfect. They'll love it. Both of them.'

Alice blushed. Janey was a newcomer to Garrison while Alice had been the driving force behind the establishment of the settlement. It had been her money that got the saloon rebuilt after the big Comanche raids back at the end of the war. It was she who had persuaded John T. McLain to stay on. She who had cajoled and bullied and loved her husband, Shawn, into building the saloon up to a size that allowed them to go into partnership with Abe Kintyre and open the general store. It had been her dream to see a town in the valley and now that dream was come true. Janey had come in with an Army patrol. Comanches had hit the wagons and left Janey's husband blank-eyed and hairless. And Alice Docherty was the only person who knew that Janey had felt no grief – couldn't, because she hadn't loved Alexander Carey. Which was why she had given her maiden name when they asked her who she was.

And in turn, Janey shared a secret of Alice's. It wasn't anything the older woman had ever admitted openly. Not even to herself: she couldn't and wouldn't. After all, she loved Shawn. What she felt for John T. McLain was what any woman would feel for a brown-eyed, handsome man with a slow Missouri drawl. It wasn't what she felt for Shawn. But if she had been younger . . . If she was McLain's own age . . .

She hid her embarrassment behind a show of interest in Janey's dress. It had come from Abe's store, subtly altered by Janey's skill with a needle – the skill that helped her make a living – and it did look good. It clung in all the right places without revealing too much: the way dresses had looked on Alice twenty years ago.

'If John T.'s interested in anyone,' she said, 'it'll be you. You look lovely.'

Janey made a small dismissive gesture: 'John T. McLain doesn't even notice me. I think he's afraid of me.'

Alice laughed. 'You've not seen him looking. Besides, I don't think that man's afraid of anything.'

'Not of men,' said Janey; almost wistfully. 'Not of bandits or Indians. Just me.'

'Makes you kinda special,' said Alice. 'Time was, I thought he'd never even look. That man's got a lot of past.'

Janey nodded. She had heard how McLain had lost his wife in the Civil War. Heard how he rode with Bloody Bill Anderson and Butcher Harvey. Heard he was a friend of Josey Wales. She had seen him use the big Dragoon he wore, going up against Zac Moffat and facing down the whole Circle Z crew. She knew he was a big, calm, confident man. Except around her. Around her something seemed to happen to him: he either got tongue-tied or lost his temper. And she was much the same, except for the tied tongue. Janey Page was seldom at a loss for words.

'Who's escorting you?' Alice asked her.

'Frank,' Janey replied. 'He asked first.'

Frank was Captain Frank Donnelly, the officer in charge of the garrison. He was a good catch, save for his rule-book attitude and – in Alice's view – his implacable dislike of McLain.

'So John T. did ask?' she murmured.

'Abe Kintyre asked,' Janey laughed. 'And Swede. And even One-Eye. But not John T. McLain.'

Alice shook her head. She felt almost ashamed of feeling vaguely pleased. 'That man,' she said. 'Times are, I think he's got no sense.'

Janey said nothing in reply and both women settled to fixing their dresses and their hair until they were satisfied with the result. Then they went out of the little cabin where Janey lived and walked down to the saloon.

Shawn Docherty was behind the bar, his face flushed by the constraint of the stiff collar he was wearing. Alice thought he didn't look at all bad in the store suit, with a tie around his neck and his cropped silver-grey hair slicked down with pomade. McLain was facing him, leaning on the bar with the coat of his suit hitched back over the butt of the Dragoon on his right hip. The suit was new, creases still showing on the pants, and McLain had obviously succumbed to Abe Kintyre's blandishments because he was wearing a new pair of boots. He was hatless, his long brown hair falling on to his collar in thick waves. His tanned face creased in a smile as the two women came in, and Alice thought again how handsome he was.

Beside him, Randall French set down his glass and raised his silver-topped walking cane in salute. French was the owner of the French Seven, a tall, thin man with prematurely grey hair. He had served with Jubal Early during the War, coming south when a Minié ball left him permanently crippled to build up the biggest spread in the territory. Bigger, now that he had bought up the old Circle Z land along with the two thousand head it carried. That many steers, joined with his own three thousand-odd, made him one of the biggest ranchers in all Texas.

'Ladies,' he said affably, 'you look radiant.'

Shawn Docherty said, 'Don't they just? The two best-lookin' wimmen in the territory.'

Janey curtsied. Alice stared at McLain.

'You got nothin' to say, John T.?'

The big man went on smiling. 'They said it all, Alice.'

'I'm not sure Mr McLain appreciates the way a lady dresses,' said Janey. And regretted it even as the words came out.

'Ain't the way she puts it on,' said Shawn. 'It's the way she . . .'

'Shawn!' Alice's voice was stern, cutting him short. The grizzled ex-sergeant grinned. 'We'll wait over there.' His wife indicated a table. 'Frank Donnelly is coming by to collect Janey.'

She glanced at McLain as she said it, wondering if the frown that crossed his face indicated jealousy.

'Sure,' said Docherty. 'You want a drink?'

'Lemonade.' Primly; ladylike.

'I ain't sure I enjoy gettin' civilized,' murmured Shawn. 'Time was I didn't need say *sorry* every time I farted.'

McLain and French chuckled, watching him fetch a jug of lemonade from under the bar. His constant arguments with his wife were a standing joke in Garrison, not quite hiding the devotion he felt.

'Well,' said French, 'this should be quite an event.'

'Yeah.' McLain nodded. 'I ain't seen no travellin' show since I was a kid.'

'More than just a travelling show.' The rancher touched the pearl stickpin in his foulard. 'Selections from Shakespeare, no less.'

McLain started to ask who Shakespeare was, but just then Frank Donnelly walked in. He was in dress blues, a sabre belted to his waist and a kepi under his arm. He glanced round, smoothing his neatly-trimmed black moustache. His eyes settled on McLain for a moment, then passed on to Janey Page. He smiled faintly, looking pleased with himself.

'The captain seems cheerful,' French remarked. 'He looks well pleased with himself.'

'Yeah.' McLain watched Donnelly sit down between Alice and Janey. 'Don't he just.'

'A pretty girl.' French followed McLain's gaze. 'I'm surprised you . . .'

He broke off as the Missouri man grunted, reaching over the bar for the bottle: at times it was best to leave McLain to his own thoughts.

Shawn Docherty came back looking at the gold watch chained across his vest.

'Nearly time.'

Outside, wagons had been brought together and planks laid over to form a stage. A canvas was strung on poles, making a backdrop painted with woodland scenes. Lanterns were already lit against the dying of the light, the funnels encased in polished metal so that the radiance was directed on to the stage. Behind, there was the big, wooden wagon that served the actors as transport and changing room. Trestles served as seats, and already there were people taking their places.

Donnelly stood up, offering his arm to Janey. Alice came over to claim Shawn. Randall French said, 'Well, John, shall we go?'

McLain nodded, holding the batwings for the limping man.

They sat down, McLain next to Janey. He caught a faint drift of perfume on the evening air and glanced at her from the corner of his eye. He was surprised to see her blush and turn her head away. Less surprised to see Donnelly's furious glare.

Winston DeVere – at least that was the name painted on the side of the wagon – came on to the stage. His hair was unnaturally black, gleaming in the lamps' light, emphasising the paleness of his made-up face. He was wearing a black doublet and black tights; a dagger hung from his waist in a silver sheath. There was a rumble of laughter.

He raised his hands to command silence.

When eventually it came, he said: 'The Winston DeVere Travelling Repertory Company is pleased to announce an evening of Shakespearean delights.'

His voice was very deep, pitched to carry. It reminded McLain of Bill Anderson shouting orders in the midst of battle.

'And to commence,' said DeVere, 'the soliloquy from *Hamlet*.'

A trooper at the rear called, 'Ham what?'

DeVere ignored the interruption. 'To be, or not to be. That is the question . . .'

McLain listened to the words, wondering if people had really talked like that once, finding himself interested despite himself. Alice had spoken of building a permanent theatre some day; when the town had grown some more, when there was enough money, enough people. He wondered if he would be around to see it.

DeVere finished his piece and there was a round of applause. It got louder as two women came on stage, wearing the kind of costumes McLain had seen in the bigger San Antonio saloons. The way they were painted up, they could have come right out of one, and McLain found himself glancing at Janey again. She looked good, her face bright as she watched the performance. McLain thought that maybe he would ask her about Shakespeare: she knew a lot about that kind of thing. It was one of the reasons he felt nervous around her. He turned back to the actors.

And then the whole thing broke down in chaos as a wagon came careening into the lamplight and threatened to collide with the stage.

McLain was on his feet before the thing had halted. He recognised the driver as Johann Koch; the woman beside him as Inge, his wife. She was holding something in her arms and her face was ugly with weeping.

Koch jumped to the ground, his bald head glistening. His eyes were wild, huge and staring, his lips moving in soundless words. He saw McLain approaching and yelled, 'McLain! My God! *Sie haben meine . . .*'

'American,' McLain grabbed the little settler and shook him. 'Speak American.'

'Mary.' Koch's voice was hoarse. 'They killed Mary. They killed my little Maria.'

McLain looked at the bundle Inge Koch was holding. It was wrapped in a blanket. The blanket was dark with blood and a small, pale foot hung limp from under the folds.

Winston DeVere said, 'May we continue?'

McLain looked at the actor. DeVere shut his mouth without saying anything more.

'Get her inside.' McLain pointed at the saloon. 'Alice, you help Inge.'

Alice and Janey helped the woman down from the wagon. She refused to let go the bundle, holding it tight against her chest, her tears spilling on to the rough blanket. She let them lead her up the steps, her husband trailing behind.

Shawn Docherty closed the doors as Donnelly began to shout orders to his men to stand alert and keep calm. Then he came inside. Shawn poured whiskey. Inge Koch sank into a chair, huddled over the body of her child. A low, guttural keening sound came from her open mouth and she kept shaking her head from side to side. Gently, Alice prised her hands clear of the bundle. McLain took it and set it on the table.

When he parted the folds, Janey Page said, 'Oh, my God!'

Shawn Docherty said, 'Jesus Christ!'

McLain just stared, his face getting ugly.

Mary Koch had been pretty. Once.

Not now.

Now her face was swollen and purpled. Her lips were puffed up, cut on broken teeth, her tongue extending black.

There was a circle of dark bruises around her throat and her blonde hair was bedraggled, thick with blood. There was more blood on what was left of her dress. Some had come from the wounds on her small breasts. Most had come from between her legs.

Frank Donnelly said, 'They raped her.'

Inge Koch screamed and began to weep uncontrolled.

'You sure got a way with words, Frank,' rasped McLain. And turned to Johann. Put an arm around the man's shaking shoulders and steered him over to the bar. Shawn Docherty gave him a glass.

Koch swallowed. Docherty poured again.

'All right.' McLain's voice was slow and calm; reassuring. 'Tell us what happened.'

'She went to pick flowers.' The settler said it slowly, carefully; picking his way through the still-unfamiliar language. 'She wanted a bouquet, so she went up the canyon to a place she knew. *Mein Gott!* She was only twelve years old!'

'I know,' said McLain. 'Then what?'

'She didn't come back.' Koch tugged at his necktie. 'We were all ready to ride in, but little Maria was not with us. Inge called her, but there was no answer. We thought she must have wandered. We got in the wagon to fetch her. And then we found her.'

He began to choke. Shawn gave him more whiskey.

'In the canyon?' McLain knew the place. Knew Mary's penchant for flowers. Knew – no, *had* known – Mary. 'You found her there?'

Koch nodded. '*Ja.* In the canyon. The flowers were all trampled down and Maria was there. All bloody. They killed her. They killed my little Maria.'

'They?' McLain asked. 'You saw them?'

Koch shook his head.

'I saw no one. Only Maria. All bloody. Where they left her.'

'Comanches,' said Donnelly. 'It must have been Comanches.'

McLain looked at the officer. Looked at the small, bloody corpse. And shook his head.

'No.'

'What?' Donnelly sounded outraged. 'Only a savage would do something like that.'

'You're right,' said McLain slowly. 'Only a savage. But not Comanches.'

Donnelly started to say something else, but Alice broke in.

'Listen to him, Frank. Close your mouth an' listen to him.'

'Comanch' would've taken her,' said McLain. 'Raised her as one of their own. She'd have been child-bearing age afore too long. They'd have taken her for a squaw. No, it wasn't Comanches.'

'Who?' wailed Koch. 'Who would have done this?'

'Animals!' Janey Page's voice was harsh. 'Only an animal would do a thing like this.'

'Yeah.' McLain nodded. 'Now I'll go hunt them.'

Chapter Two

The Koch place was cut back into a low ridge that spread down from the canyon walls. Beyond it the land rose in a broad, vee-shaped fan, timbered along the rimrock and grassed where the terrain flattened out. McLain rode slow past the soddy, right hand close to the Dragoon holstered on his waist. His eyes moved steadily from side to side, scanning the ground for sign of tracks other than the wheel ruts left by Koch's wagon.

He reached the place at the end where the flowers grew and dismounted. It was close on noon and the sun was shining directly down into the canyon. Over to the western side there was a blaze of colour from the cholla and prairie roses, all pink and scarlet. It reminded him of Mary's body. The flowers were crushed down over a wide area, petals strewn and broken, some showing blood dark against the scarlet. He hunkered down, staring at the earth. It was soft enough here that footprints showed clear. Deep indentations. Heel marks. Two sets.

They were not the marks a Comanche moccasin would make.

McLain followed them, letting a picture form in his mind.

There had been two men. White men. They had come down from the rimrock: horse droppings showed where they had left their animals. They must have seen Mary picking flowers and approached her. The way the tracks were indented, it looked like she had run. They had chased her. Caught her. Killed her.

But first they had raped her.

McLain spat, his mouth tasting sour.

Up on the rimrock the tracks of two shod horses wound

through the timber. McLain followed them westwards, but after an hour – maybe more – they got lost on hard ground. He cursed, obscenities flowing in condemnation. It was just as Janey had said: animals. And like animals, they had gone to ground. It would, he thought, take an Indian to trail them.

And the thought gave him an idea.

A wild idea.

Crazy.

But the best he had.

Back in the canyon he saw a column of blue-clad figures riding hard for the Koch place. He reined in, recognising Frank Donnelly in the lead.

'You don't waste time.' There was grudging admiration in the captain's voice. 'Find anything?'

'Tracks,' said McLain. 'Two men. Both white.'

'How can you know that?' Donnelly demanded.

'Shit, Frank!' McLain's pent-up rage came close to boiling over. 'The bastards were wearing boots. You can see the heel marks up where the girl was killed. They was ridin' shod horses. You ever know a Comanch' to wear boots?'

Donnelly shrugged, unwilling to give up his original assumption. 'I'll take a look around myself. Make a sweep of the area.'

McLain stared at him. Then: 'You do that, Frank. You go waste some time.'

Donnelly's good-looking features got ugly for a moment, then he checked his temper.

'Which way did they go?'

'West,' said McLain. 'The tracks peter out in the badlands. Ain't no way I can follow them.'

'I don't give up so easily,' said Donnelly; smug.

McLain didn't bother replying. Just watched as the officer raised his arm to wave the column forwards, then slammed his heels against his animal's sides and lifted the big bay gelding up to a gallop.

It was full dark before he got back to Garrison. All the festive feeling had gone out of the place, replaced by an ugly mood that was getting stoked up in the saloon. The makeshift stage had been removed and the DeVere troupe was clustered around two tables, somehow cut off from the inhabitants. Randall French had gone back to his spread, leaving word that if McLain needed to raise a posse he had only to ask.

McLain grunted when Alice told him, and said: 'A posse? I can't raise no posse. I ain't even a lawman.'

'You're the closest thing we got,' Alice replied. 'You find anything?'

McLain nodded and told her about the tracks.

'What you gonna do?'

'Find them,' he answered. There was a certainty in his voice that didn't allow for doubt or argument. 'Find them an' kill them.'

'You mustn't do that.' Janey Page came out from one of the rooms at the back, where the Dochertys had built on. 'That would make you a killer.'

'Thought you had me marked that way already,' he said.

She shook her head. 'You use your guns too easily, Mr McLain. But I don't think you're a killer.'

Once again she had him confused. He took the whiskey Shawn offered him and asked, 'What am I, then?'

'Like Alice said: the nearest thing Garrison has to a lawman. It should be made legal.'

McLain frowned. 'Me? A Peace Officer?'

'Why not?' She looked at him, a challenge in her clear blue eyes. 'You already do the job, near as makes no difference. Why not make it legal? Make it a proper appointment.'

'That,' said Alice, 'is one helluva good idea.'

'Lady,' said McLain, 'I don't have the time. You'd need papers from San Antonio. An' then folks might not welcome a Johnny Reb as their marshal.'

'I think they would,' said Janey. 'I know they would.'

'Seconded,' smiled Alice.

'First, I got things to do.' McLain emptied his glass. 'Like finding who killed Mary.'

'Was something Inge said,' Shawn Docherty recalled, 'might help. Seems Mary was wearing a necklace. Silver links. It wasn't on her.'

McLain nodded. 'Mighta got ripped off. I didn't see nothin' like that, though.'

'So could be the killers took it,' Shawn opined. 'Be a way of spottin' them.'

'If you can find them,' said Alice. 'How you figger to do that?'

McLain smiled. It wasn't a pleasant expression. 'I got an idea. I'll need some stuff from the store.'

'Help yoreself.' Alice stared at him curiously. 'What you got in mind?'

McLain went on smiling: 'Best you don't know. Frank wouldn't like it, an' he still thinks he's runnin' this place.'

'If you find them,' Janey Page asked, 'will you kill them?'

McLain looked at her. He was suddenly confused: he didn't understand what she was getting at. He said, 'What the hell else would I do? You saw Mary's body. You know what they did.'

'A Peace Officer wouldn't kill them,' she replied. 'Not like that. Not out of hand.'

'All right.' McLain felt irritation rising along with the confusion. 'You tell me what else I do.'

'Bring them in,' said Janey. 'For trial. Make it legal. Proper.'

McLain snorted, putting down his glass. 'We got no judge. We held a trial, it wouldn't be legal.'

'Besides,' said Shawn, 'there wouldn't be no doubt about the verdict. Folks here would have them strung up soon as spit.'

'Not if Mr McLain acted as Peace Officer,' said the girl. 'We could make it proper. Form a Citizens' Committee.'

'Yeah.' Alice nodded. 'We'd need something like that, anyway. If we're to have a proper town.'

'She's got a point,' murmured Shawn. 'She could be right.'

'Hell!' McLain turned for the door. 'I'll try it your way. I ain't making no promises, but if I can I'll bring them in. Alive.'

Without waiting for them to say anything more he went out of the saloon and into the store. What Janey had said made sense in a curious kind of way. He was the nearest thing Garrison had to a lawman, but that position was one of unspoken acceptance on both sides. It wasn't anything he had looked for, just a thing that had come about gradually, without anyone thinking much about it. Frank Donnelly kept his men disciplined – some would say too disciplined – but civilian disputes either got settled on the spot, or sorted out by McLain. Someone had to do it, and he was handy enough with his fists and his guns to back the natural authority of his size. Nothing official, just something that had happened. The same way people looked to Alice or Shawn as leaders of the community, kind of unofficial mayors. And if the place went on growing, then a regular lawman – a legalised, appointed lawman – would be needed. There were a lot more people drifting down to southern Texas now, and the only way Garrison would grow into a regular town would be by following the rules. So maybe Janey was right. She had that irritating habit of seeing things other folks couldn't.

So maybe he should play it her way.

'You look angry, John.' Abe Kintyre lifted his wiry frame off his rocker and ran a hand through his curly hair. 'You lose them?'

McLain nodded. 'But I'm gonna find them. Need some stuff to do it, though.'

'Help yourself.' Kintyre spread his arms to embrace the trade goods stacked around the room. 'Anything to find Mary's killers.'

'Thanks, Abe.' McLain began to list his needs.

A dozen hand axes.

A dozen blankets. The brightest in stock.

A box of trinkets: necklaces, ear-rings; bright baubles.

A dozen knives.

Kintyre gathered the stuff with curiosity spreading clearer over his wrinkled face. He decided it was better not to ask what McLain had in mind.

'One more thing.' The big Missouri man halted at the door. 'Be best you didn't say anything about this. Especially not to Donnelly.'

Kintyre nodded. 'Sure, John.'

McLain went out, walking fast to the corral behind the saloon. The bay gelding greeted him with a snicker of welcome, but he pushed the big horse away: it had done enough running. Instead, he put his saddle on a grey; a tall, deep-chested stallion the Dochertys had collected from a travelling gambler whose skill with a pistol hadn't quite matched his talent for dealing off the bottom of the deck.

He led the horse round to the front of the store and loaded the sacks behind the saddle. Then he mounted up and heeled the grey to a fast canter, heading west.

He splashed through the shallow waters of the Rio Verde and rode over the moonlit grass. Ahead of his path the hills bulked dark and menacing, the moon not yet high enough to illuminate the rimrock. He reached the foothills and made camp. What he planned to do called for daylight. Perhaps for a well-rested horse. One that could run fast without tiring.

He ate jerked beef and biscuits, washing it down with water from his canteen. Then he stretched on his blanket and went to sleep with the two big Dragoon pistols laid beside him.

It was a wild idea.

And still the only one he had.

He woke while the sky was still grey, the night not yet driven off by the sun. Over to the east a pale yellow glow showed along the horizon, becoming brighter as he ate and stowed the sacks back on the stallion. It was still no more than a promise as he mounted again and pushed deeper into the hills.

Beyond the rim the land became flat, grass stretching in a waving green sea to the far-off line of the Eagle range. Ahead, shimmering in the now-risen sun, a mesa stuck from the flat, its walls golden and red. He reached it as the sun climbed to its zenith, and halted. There were cracks in the surface like the lines on a man's face, aeons of sun and wind and storm etching age into the stone. Some were deep enough that a horse might comfortably enter, and he walked the grey stallion inside one of the largest. He tethered the animal and carried the sacks back to the entrance. Then he checked the load in the big Sharps and the chambers of the Dragoons. By habit, he carried the two pistols on empty chambers, not wishing to risk accidental discharge. Now he dropped the new linen cartridges that came with powder and ball complete in a single load into the empty chambers. Greased the frontal holes, and then set percussion caps carefully over the nipples. He dropped one pistol into the holster on his right hip and stuck the second through his belt. Then he began to gather sticks from the litter around the mesa's foot.

He piled the dry wood a little way from the entrance to the split and struck a match. When the dry wood was burning, he layered fresher, greener pieces over the flames. Soon a thin column of dark smoke was lifting vertically into the still, windless air.

McLain sat down with his back to the rock and the sacks of trade goods spread out in front on one of the blankets. His mouth was very dry and the hair on the back of his neck seemed to prickle.

He began to wonder if the idea was too crazy to work.

And then the first Comanche showed.

He came out of the heat haze dancing along the crest of a

rise. His hair was long and black, held off his flat, broad-nosed face by a leather band that held three eagle feathers. He carried a lance, and around his waist there was a belt into which was thrust a stone club. His mustang carried feathers in its mane and paint on the chest and flanks.

He halted, staring at McLain. Then raised the lance. Seven more warriors topped the rise and halted in a line.

McLain climbed to his feet. He left the Sharps propped against the stone as he raised both arms high above his head. His hands were empty, palms outwards. The dryness in his mouth was scorching now. The prickling at the back of his neck was an irritation he longed to scratch. He ignored both, standing there very still. Waiting.

The Comanches rode forwards.

Chapter Three

In their own language the Comanche called themselves *Nemenna*. It meant, *The People*. Comanche was a name given them by the Utes. It had stuck because it fitted. It meant, 'the people who fight us all the time'. They were renowned for their ferocity, for their uncompromising hostility towards anyone claiming land they regarded as their own. They fought with the Apache and the Osage, with the Tonkawa and the Pawnee and the Ute. And with the white settlers. They were superb horsemen – some called them the Cossacks of the Plains – and their reputation for cruelty was unsurpassed.

As the eight riders came steadily towards him, McLain wondered again if he was crazy.

They came down the rise at an easy canter, the lances still lifted to the sky. McLain saw that all carried stone clubs or hatchets; only two wore metal knives in their belts. The dryness in his mouth became a burning irritation that seared his throat and made him want to spit. Instead, he kept his mouth closed, staring fixedly at the leader. If the lance dropped, that would be the signal: confirmation of his madness.

He waited.

The leader reined in, lance still pointing skywards. He peered at McLain with eyes too dark to show any expression. Shouted something in his own language.

McLain smiled. It was an effort to stretch his lips back over his teeth. He lowered his arms slowly, indicating the trade goods spread at his feet.

He said, '*Buenas dias.*'

It sounded stupid. Meaningless.

He struggled to recall the Spanish he had picked up from Gomez and his whores. Back in Garrison. Back in safety.

He said, '*Amigo. Yo soy amigo.*'

The Comanche laughed. A harsh sound that seemed to echo off the walls of the mesa. To ring inside McLain's head. He called something to his companions and they came in closer, fanning out so that they spread in a semi-circle facing McLain.

'*Ingles?*' he said. '*Hablan Ingles?*'

One of the Indians said, '*Poco*. A little.'

McLain switched to his own language, speaking slowly; carefully. Lacing it with Spanish.

'I want to trade.'

He stooped to pick up an axe, lifting it so that the sun glittered off the metal head. The Comanches stared at the blade. He picked up a knife. A Bowie, with a twelve-inch blade and a brass guard. He walked slowly towards the horsemen, holding out the weapons.

'For you. Trade.'

'For what?' The Comanches' eyes were fixed on the axe and the knife. McLain thought he saw greed on their faces.

'We talk,' McLain said. Wondering if his voice was as hoarse as it sounded to him. 'We talk trade.'

One of the Indians grunted something that sounded like *Comanchero*. The leader shook his head; said something in reply.

'You are the one killed many,' said the spokesman.

McLain kept the smile fixed on his face with conscious effort.

'We fought,' he said. 'The Comanche are warriors.'

The leader grunted again and swung clear of his mustang. He walked up to McLain, looking small now that he was on the ground. A heavily-muscled man with short, bowed legs. Still deadly.

McLain held out the knife and the axe. 'For you.'

The Comanche took them. Tested the Bowie on his

thumb. Laughed as blood trickled. He stuck the knife in his belt and swung the axe a few times, whistling through the air. Then he called to the others and they dismounted, grouping around the blanket. Staring at the goods.

'What want?'

McLain began to explain. It wasn't easy, not in a mixture of English and Spanish and sign language. He spoke slowly, carefully, pausing now and then to scratch marks in the soil, trying to show them the location of the Koch homestead, to make them understand what it was he wanted.

Finally he seemed to get the idea across: the leader grunted and the spokesman said, 'These for men?'

McLain nodded.

'Firesticks better.' The Indian pointed at the Dragoons. 'Give firesticks.'

McLain shook his head.

There was a brief discussion. The Comanches stared at the white man. They began to laugh.

The one translating said, 'You brave. Like Nemenna. Show how brave. Fight for firesticks. You win, we help you. You lose, we take firesticks.'

McLain nodded: he didn't have much other choice.

The Indians stood up.

'Get horse.'

McLain went into the split in the rock and fetched the grey out. Seven of the Comanches were standing, leaning on their lances. One was mounted. He looked younger than the others. There were no feathers in his hair and his quill breastplate was plainer, less decorated. He was holding his lance in his right hand, the stone tip angled down. One of his companions tossed a lance to McLain.

The man from Missouri caught it, seeing now what they expected. It was a game. A cruel game: Comanche against white man; using lances. The favoured weapon of the Nemenna. He had seen the poles in action. Seen how the warriors could use them to gut an enemy, leaving him unhorsed with his belly ripped open, entrails dripping from the point of the lance.

But he didn't have any other choice. Not now.

He got up on the grey.

'No firesticks,' said the spokesman. 'Use firesticks and we kill.'

McLain nodded. He hefted the lance, finding the point of balance. The pole was around ten feet long, of some fire-hardened wood. The tip was chipped stone, fastened to the pole with rawhide thongs. Where he held the thing there was more rawhide, wound round to give a grip. A single feather, dyed red and black, fluttered at the head. McLain couched the lance under his right arm, imitating the mounted Indian.

The warrior backed his horse, measuring off a distance that would be sufficient for the mustang to reach its full speed by the time it reached McLain. The white man grinned tightly and walked the stallion back. The grey was a lot bigger than the stringy little Indian pony and over a distance could most likely reach a greater speed, but it needed more distance to achieve its full pace. The mustang would be swifter over a short run, reaching full gallop almost instantaneously and turning a whole lot tighter. The Indians expected that. Expected to see McLain gutted so they could take his guns.

He hoped he could win.

Hoped they would honour their side of the bargain if he did.

If he lost it wouldn't matter any more. Nothing would. To him.

The Comanche screamed and slammed his moccasins against the pony's painted flanks. The smaller animal surged forwards, nostrils flaring. McLain remembered the times he had ridden with Anderson and Butcher Harvey. Reins looped about the saddlehorn and the Dragoons spitting flame in both hands. He hoped the grey would respond the same way as he swung the leather around the horn and drove his heels hard against the horse's sides.

As he expected, the stallion was slower to respond than the mustang. He saw the Comanche closing in with the lance rising to parallel the pony's chest. Saw it lift as the warrior adjusted the angle to compensate for the grey's greater height. And he leant over in the saddle, forgetting his own lance as the Indian's sliced air three inches from his right thigh.

He smashed his right heel against the stallion's flank, willing the big horse to turn, steering with his knees as he clutched at the saddlehorn and fought down the temptation to haul out a Dragoon and blast the Comanche from his pad saddle.

The mustang turned tighter. It was already coming back in as the grey came round. McLain rode head on into the charge, bringing up his lance to point on the warrior's belly. The Comanche whooped, his face fierce, flattening over his mount's neck. McLain went sideways again, feeling his shirt rip as pain burnt a line down his side. He ignored it, conscious only of the need to turn and face the charge again before the Indian drove the lance in through his back.

This time the grey came round faster. It seemed to sense McLain's urgency, pulling out reserves of agility in answer to its rider's need. It was facing the mustang as the brave closed for the third time, charging down on the smaller animal as though it sought to ride it down and crush it under its own greater weight. McLain thrust his pole forwards, stabbing it at the Indian's belly. Trying more to put off the Comanche's aim than do any real damage.

The Indian ducked under the thrust and McLain felt the tip of his lance score a second line over his ribs.

The Indian whooped and the white man heard confidence in the cry. Amusement, too. And suddenly he realised the brave was playing with him. He could have taken him on any of the charges. Had chosen not to because he wanted to show off his skill. Wanted to toy with the presumptuous white man like a cat teasing a mouse.

McLain's teeth gritted hard together. Briefly, he saw the watching Indians. Saw they were smiling. And decided to change his tactics. Instead of turning the grey, he urged the horse straight on, running away from the return gallop of the warrior. He let it go out on to the grass, gaining distance before he swung it round and turned to face the young brave.

The Comanche was still smiling. Shouting something that brought a roar of laughter from the others. McLain dug his heels against the grey's ribs, his mouth opening to let loose the old Rebel yell, the high-pitched, screaming ululation that had carried the Missouri guerrillas into battle. He gripped the stallion firmer with his knees, bringing his left hand over to grasp the lance so that he held it in both hands like a club. He reversed the thing, trailing the heavier rearward end over his shoulder. Surprise showed on the Comanche's face as the charge closed the distance between them. And then they were together, the Indian's lance driving at McLain's groin.

The big man twisted in the saddle, turning his whole body as he leant over and back. Watching the Indian's pole go floating past his belly. Swinging his own round in a terrific two-handed blow. It caught the Comanche across the chest, rattling off the quill breastplate hard enough that the brave was thrown back over the mustang's haunches. He grunted, fighting to regain his seat. And McLain turned the grey again, fast enough this time that he was facing the Indian as the mustang gathered speed.

The smile was gone from the brave's face now. Replaced with an ugly determination that exploded in a cloud of crimson as McLain shifted his weight and took the grey past the mustang on the left side. The Comanche's lance cut empty air, but McLain's – swung like a club – came round and over to smash against the bridge of his nose. There was the dull sound of bone crushing. Crimson fountained from the nostrils as the Indian's nose was flattened over his wide cheekbones. The paint on his face was lost under the spillage and he rolled back, fighting to stay astride the mustang.

McLain spun the stallion in its own length, this time catching the Comanche as he turned. He swung the lance again, thudding it over the warrior's back so that the man was hurled forwards on to the mustang's neck, a broad red bruise erupting across his shoulders.

The white man went on turning his own horse, staying in close to the Indian so that he was denied a chance to gain distance in which to use the lance effectively. McLain pounded at his shoulders and head, holding the lance one-handed now, his left grabbing the saddlehorn to aid his balance. The warrior shouted something, then closed his mouth as the butt of McLain's lance rammed into the hole, sharding teeth. He dropped his lance, reaching for the stone-headed hatchet tucked into his belt. But before he could lift the weapon, McLain rammed the butt into his face again, pulping the lips back over the broken teeth. The hatchet swung uselessly through the air, and the white man brought the lance back, spinning it to reverse his grip.

He was still close to the mustang, the grey stallion screaming in rage and panic, teeth snapping viciously at the smaller animal. He brought his arm back. Then forwards, driving the lance at the Comanche's belly.

The Indian tried to deflect the pole, but it went under his swinging arm, stabbing at his stomach. The tip struck flesh just below the breastplate. It drove through, tearing into the muscle then into the softer insides. The Comanche's mouth opened in a great gasp of sucking breath. Pain showed in his dark eyes. McLain twisted the lance, sawing it deeper into the warrior's intestines as he pushed the stallion harder against the pony. The flesh circling the entry point puckered like sucking lips. The Indian let go the hatchet, bringing both his hands over to grasp the pole driving deep through his stomach. Blood slickened his grip and the lance tore in further. McLain felt it grate on bone, then felt it push free. It stuck out from the warrior's back, the tip bloody, streamers of intestine hanging from the chipped stone.

McLain swung the grey in a circle. The lance dragged against the edges of the awful wound. The Comanche screamed, his body trembling in agony. The white man's circling movement dragged him off the mustang's back and McLain let go of the lance, watching as the brave tumbled on to the grass.

He landed on his side, the lance protruding from his belly and back. His moccasins dug against the ground, twisting him in a circle that left great swathes of crimson slick on the green. Somehow he got up on his knees. He wrapped both hands around the pole and tried to drag it free. He succeeded only in opening the wound wider, like a gaping red mouth. Blood erupted in thick spurts and cords of yellow and black gut hung from the hole. He opened his mouth, a high, rattling sound coming out that turned into a choking, sobbing noise. His body stiffened, the back straightening, then arching over. His long hair hung down far enough that it touched the tip of the lance and got bloody. Then the noise ended as he pitched forwards, hands still tight on the lance, driving the butt against the ground so that for a moment he knelt, staring at the ruin of his belly before he slumped sideways and was still.

McLain turned to face the others. He unwound the reins, calming the grey, letting his right hand hang close to the holstered Dragoon.

The Comanches were no longer laughing. Instead, they were staring wide-eyed at their dead companion. The game had not ended the way they had expected. McLain waited for them to move. To say something. To do something. He had the advantage now: he was mounted and armed. He could kill them before they could reach their ponies.

The leader looked at him, surprise fading from his dark face to be replaced with something that looked like admiration. He spoke fast in his own tongue, then nodded, pointing at McLain.

The one who spoke English came a step forwards.

'You won.'

'Yeah.' McLain held distance between them, not wanting to give the man a chance to grab for the horse. Maybe pull him down. 'I won.'

'We trade,' said the Comanche. 'You keep the firesticks.'

There was regret in his voice.

'You will help me find the men?' McLain asked. 'The two who killed the girl?'

'We will help.' The Comanche nodded. 'You fight good.'

McLain took a deep breath and let it out slow. Suddenly he was aware of the pain in his side. Hell, he thought, maybe I ain't so crazy after all. At least it worked.

Chapter Four

Where the Comanche's lance had scored his side there was a dull, throbbing pain. He had cleansed the wounds as best he could, and bandaged them. He hoped there was no infection. Hoped he would not become feverish, unable to ride. There was, at best, only a tenuous peace between him and the warriors of the Nemenna, and he knew that if he should show weakness the braves would not hesitate to turn on him. Kill him, and take the coveted guns.

He followed them, teeth gritted as he fought down the urge to scratch at the fiery throbbing.

The sun was up high and they were riding fast, strung out in a staggered line that took them westwards over the grasslands. McLain had shown them where Mary Koch had been murdered and the Indians had grunted in surprise as he explained that she was only twelve years old. The one who spoke English had said, 'White men stupid. Why kill? Make wife.' The others had spat to express their disgust. McLain, too, had spat, feeling in that moment close to the braves. They had gone up on to the rimrock and McLain had shown them where the killers had left their horses. The Indians had studied the ground and then spread out through the trees, grouping on the one who whooped and pointed with his lance to where a stream cut down from the higher ground. Sign of a camp fire showed there and the Comanches had ridden out like a pack of hunting dogs.

They had been on the trail for three days, moving west and north and west again. Following sign McLain could not see, moving steadily further from the Rio Verde valley into the wild country where southern Texas bordered with Mexico.

They halted on a bluff overlooking the Pecos River. A wide sweep of water curved in an ox-bow around a little town, slightly larger than Garrison.

The Comanche pointed and said, 'There. Men down there.'

Without saying anything more they turned their ponies and rode away.

McLain watched them go, knowing that if they should ever meet again they would try to kill him. The peace was ended; the bargain made. Honour was satisfied. He rode towards the town.

Frank Donnelly said, 'He's crazy. What does he hope to find?'

'The men who killed Mary,' said Alice Docherty; bluntly.

'They're long gone,' grunted Donnelly. 'They could be anywhere.'

'He'll find them,' Alice said. There was certainty in her voice.

Donnelly shrugged and said, 'How?'

'I don't know,' answered the grey-haired woman. 'But he will.'

'Not alone,' said Donnelly. 'Not unless he gets himself a tracker.'

Alice looked at him with a faint smile curving the edges of her mouth. She said nothing.

McLain walked the grey stallion past the sign planted in the earth a few hundred yards out of the town. The pole was leant over, the plank nailed to the top scoured by wind and sun. The words burnt into the wood were faded, but he could still read the name: *Schotter's Crossing*. There was a livery stable and a general store; a smithy, a hardware store and a dry goods store; a mission building that looked like it hadn't been opened in a long time; a saloon. He dismounted outside the livery.

An old man with a battered hat with Confederate insignia at the front climbed slowly to his feet.

'Look like you come a ways.'

McLain nodded, then: 'You got a doctor here?'

The old man grinned as he heard the Missouri accent. 'Tod Sloane, friend. Runs the saloon. Where you from?'

His own voice was a slow, Southern drawl.

McLain said, 'Garrison. Over to the Rio Verde.'

'Before,' said the old man. 'Home.'

'Home's Garrison,' said McLain. 'Before that, Missouri.'

'Welcome.' The old man took the grey's reins. 'Me, I hail from Richmond. Served with Mosby. You?'

'Anderson,' said McLain. 'Anderson an' Harvey.'

'Met Harvey once,' said the old man. 'Ugly feller.'

'He had his good points.' McLain slung his saddlebags over his left shoulder, wincing as the movement shifted the bandages. 'Good man to have on your side.'

'Yeah.' The old man pointed at McLain's side. McLain saw that three fingers were missing from his hand. 'You hurt?'

'Why I need a doctor.'

'Comanche?' asked the oldster, adding when the man from Missouri nodded, 'Goddam bastards.'

'They got their points, too,' grunted McLain.

'Looks like they made 'em.' The old man grinned. 'On you.'

'Yeah.' McLain fetched coins from his pocket. 'There been anyone through lately?'

The old man's grin faded, his face going blank.

'Maybe. Maybe not. Why?'

McLain tossed him a coin. A dollar.

'Be two men. Maybe scratched.'

'Don't pay to ask too many questions.' The old man's face stayed blank. 'Don't pay to answer 'em, either.'

A second coin glinted in the warm air. Disappeared inside the old man's vest.

'Why'd you be askin'?' He scratched his stubbled cheek. 'If they was here.'

'They killed someone,' McLain said. 'A girl.'

'Yours?'

McLain shook his head. 'She was twelve years old. They raped her.'

'Christ!' The oldster shook his head. 'An' they say Mosby was bad.'

'Well?' McLain was getting impatient. 'You seen them?'

'You law?' countered the old man. 'I don't see no badge.'

'Don't have one,' said McLain. 'Kind of, I guess.'

'All right.' The old man came to a decision. 'Don't tell no one I told you, but there was two fellers come in a few days back. One had marks on his face. Tall man. Around yore size. Yellow hair. The other was smaller. Pockmarked face. They holed up in the saloon.'

McLain nodded, unshipping the Sharps. 'Thanks.'

'Remember,' said the old man. 'I never told you.'

McLain grunted and turned away.

He walked down the street to the saloon. It was a single-storey building with a flat roof and glassless windows set either side of the batwings. There was a bar running the length of one wall, planks set on barrels. It was hot and dark and musty, the atmosphere redolent of sweat and cheap liquor. Behind the bar there was a tall, thin man with a tousled mop of lank black hair and a long, greasy moustache. He looked up as McLain came in.

The man from Missouri asked, 'You Tod Sloane?'

The barkeep nodded, and McLain said: 'The old man at the stable said you doctored folks.'

Sloane grinned. 'Folks an' horses, friend. What's the trouble?'

'Comanche lance,' said McLain. 'You want to take a look?'

Sloane shrugged and pointed to a chair. There was no one else in the place.

McLain sat down and opened his shirt. Sloane peeled away the bandages, eyes narrowing as he saw the wounds. Without speaking, he went back to the bar, reaching over to fetch out a bottle of clear liquid and a cloth that didn't look clean.

'This'll sting some.'

McLain winced as the man splashed the liquid over the torn flesh. Sloane wiped the dried blood away and poured more of the liquid. It burned worse than the original wounding. Still without speaking, Sloane fetched cloths and wound them around the big man's ribs. McLain buttoned his shirt and stood up.

'Thanks.'

'One dollar,' said Sloane. His voice was dry, whispery. 'Keep the bandage on a few days. You should live.'

McLain nodded. 'I'll take a bottle an' a room.'

'Dollar apiece,' said Sloane. 'One meal thrown in.'

McLain dropped two dollars on the bar. 'Everything a dollar here?' he asked.

'One horse town,' said Sloane. 'One horse, one dollar. I hafta make a livin'.'

'Yeah.' McLain sipped the whiskey. It burned his insides the same way the other liquid had burned his side. 'You get many folks comin' through?'

'Some.' Sloane shrugged. 'Enough.'

'Two men,' McLain said. 'Big man with yellow hair. The other's got pockmarks.'

Sloane's eyes flickered towards the end of the room. There was a door there. He said, 'I don't want no trouble.'

'You won't get none.' McLain put his glass down. 'So long as you stay outta my way.'

'You ain't law,' said Sloane. 'What you want them for?'

'Rape,' said McLain. 'An' murder.'

'I only got yore word on that.' Sloane's hands went under the bar. 'You could be lyin'.'

'Yeah,' said McLain, 'but I ain't. They killed a girl. She was twelve years old.'

Sloane shrugged. 'All right. The door at the end. Last room down.'

'Thanks.' McLain tapped the bar. 'Don't butt in.'

Sloane's hands came up with a shotgun in them. The barrels were cut down to around eighteen inches. He grinned. 'Don't cotton to child-killers, friend. Reckoned to help you.'

'I need it, I'll holler.' McLain eased the Dragoon clear of the holster. 'I want them alive.'

Sloane frowned. 'Why? Kill 'em here.'

'No.' McLain shook his head. 'I gave someone my word.'

'They're mean,' said Sloane.

'So'm I,' McLain grunted. 'Stay clear.'

He went down to the rear of the saloon and opened the door. It gave way to a covered porch facing on to a row of shacks, no more than rooms with tar-paper roofs and windowless walls. The boards creaked under his boots and a scrawny chicken scuttled from his path. A woman with bright red lips marked by little sores smiled at him. McLain ignored her and she spat behind his back. The sun filtered down through the cracks in the porch, making bars of alternating light and shadow. Dust motes spun in the air. There was a smell of rotting food.

McLain reached the end of the porch and halted. He looked at the door of the shack. It was hinged on two strips of leather nailed to the wood, latched with a hank of cord. He snapped the hammer of the Dragoon back and brought his right foot up, kicking forwards.

The door flew loose from the hinges, crashing inwards. The woman screamed. McLain went through the gap, the pistol swinging to cover the darkness inside.

There were two men. One was stripped to the waist, sitting at a small table with a glass in his hands. The other was stretched on the bed, fully clothed. He had curly black hair and his face was pitted with smallpox scars. The one at the table had yellow hair. There were scratches on his face.

'Don't!' McLain's shout halted the yellow-haired man's hand a few inches from the Starr holstered on his waist. The pockmarked man sat up.

'Who the hell are you?'

He sounded calm.

'Name's McLain,' said the big man. 'I come from Garrison.'

'What the hell you want?' The voice had a West Texas twang: nasal. It didn't sound at all worried. 'Where's Garrison?'

The blond man sniffed and lifted the glass, staring from McLain to his companion.

'Rio Verde valley,' said McLain. 'Where you killed the girl.'

The pockmarked man grinned and said, 'What girl?'

'Mary Koch.' McLain kept the Dragoon pointed between the two. 'The one you raped.'

The pockmarked man went on grinning. 'Prove it.'

McLain pointed with his left hand at the scratches on the blond's cheek. Four long furrows that ran from the cheekbone to the jawline. He wondered why he didn't just gun them: and thought of Janey Page. And cursed her for tying his hands with words.

'Ran into chaparral,' said the pockmarked man. 'You ain't law.'

'Near as makes no difference.' McLain began to think that a badge could be useful. 'Stand up.'

'Big difference west of the Pecos,' said the man, still not moving. Just resting back with hands behind his head. Smiling as though McLain's presence was a welcome break from the boredom of the room. 'You ain't got no authority.'

'I got this.' McLain gestured with the Dragoon.

'I got friends.' The man brought his hands into view. 'In Schotter's Crossing.'

McLain saw something silvery glinting on his wrist: a

thread of fine metal links, wound twice around the tanned skin. Shawn Docherty had said something about a necklace.

He said, 'I gave my word I'd try to bring you in alive. I could forget that.'

The pockmarked man laughed. 'You was goin' to kill us, friend, you'd have done it. I don't think you got the stomach.'

Anger exploded inside McLain. He wished he hadn't given his word. Wished he could break it. He squeezed the trigger of the Dragoon.

Inside the room muzzle flash shone brighter than the sun. The reek of black powder replaced the smell of decaying food. The blond man shouted something that was lost under the roar of the pistol. Splinters flew from the wall two inches right of the pockmarked man's face. A round hole appeared in the wood. Down the porch a woman screamed again.

'Christ!' The pockmarked man came upright, swinging his feet on to the floor.

McLain hauled the hammer back.

'You ready? You get the message?'

Both men nodded. McLain said, 'Unfasten yore belts.'

The Starr dropped on to the boards, followed by the Colt's Navy the pockmarked man was wearing.

McLain said, 'Put yore shirt on.'

The blond pulled a faded red shirt over his brawny shoulders. His big blue eyes stared at McLain with a bovine blankness. The man from Missouri couldn't tell if it was indifference or whiskey or stupidity. He backed out the door.

'Come through slow. Keep yore hands where I can see them.'

They came out on to the porch. The woman with the sores on her mouth ducked back inside her room. A raven-haired woman stared curiously. Sloane came out with the shotgun in his hands.

'Point that someplace else,' McLain called.

Sloane went back into the saloon.

He was standing just inside the door as they went through. The pockmarked man glared at him and said, 'You're a bastard, Tod.'

Sloane shrugged and answered, 'Accident of birth, Ben. You, you're a self-made man.'

The blond stared at Sloane. He sniffed again, turning his heavy head to glance at Ben. The pockmarked man nodded and ducked forwards from the waist. As he moved, his left leg shot out, heel slamming against the door so that it swung back in McLain's face. The Dragoon blasted a single shot that ricocheted off the metal lock as the Missouri man was thrown off stride. Then the door was dragged to, and he heard the lock snap into place.

Sloane gasped and the blond grabbed the shotgun. He got both big hands on the barrels and wrenched the thing upwards. Sloane's finger was drawn tight against the forwards trigger, slipping the hammer. The shotgun detonated. The left-hand barrel ploughed a swathe of buckshot upwards into the blond man's face. It was ten-gauge. It stripped the flesh from the underside of the jaw and blew the bone through the roof of the mouth. Bone and teeth and tongue were blasted into the hole. The top of the skull exploded, the blond hair lifting in a halo around the shattered cranium, becoming abruptly red as blood and sticky, grey brain matter fountained out and up. The eyes blew from the sockets and for an instant Sloane was staring into two red gaps. Then his own vision was lost under the flood of crimson that washed over his face.

The pockmarked man shoved the blond, toppling the corpse into the barkeep. Sloane screamed and let go the scattergun, falling under the deadweight. Spitting as pieces of brain dripped into his mouth.

The man called Ben grabbed the shotgun and triggered the second barrel into the door.

McLain spun sideways as a gaping hole was blasted around the lock. He kicked the door, hurling through as it swung open. Sloane was down on the floor screaming in raw terror as he struggled to push the dead man from him. Ben was behind the bar, thumbing paper cartridges into the scattergun. He snapped the breech closed as McLain came through. Bottles exploded, sending splinters of glass and streamers of whiskey across the room. McLain went down in a long dive, triggering the Dragoon. His shot splintered wood from the front of the bar. Then Ben was on his feet and running through the batwings.

McLain cursed and followed him on to the street.

There were people watching now. Ducking back inside the stores as Ben moved slowly towards the livery. McLain saw he was holding spare cartridges in his left hand. Had the shotgun loaded again.

'Stay back!' The pockmarked face was ugly. 'You move, you get both barrels. Like the girl.'

He sniggered. And McLain cursed.

Cursed Janey Page.

Cursed the promise he had made.

Cursed Ben.

Cursed the shotgun.

Cursed his own stupidity.

He backed into the saloon, holstering the Dragoon. The Sharps was where he had left it, on the bar. He picked it up and thumbed the hammer back, moving fast for the door.

Ben was half-way down the street, heading for the livery.

McLain brought the buffalo gun up to his shoulder. Sighted as he sucked in a deep breath. Squeezed the trigger as he let it out. The Sharps kicked hard against his shoulder, flame and powder smoke gouting from the muzzle.

The heel of Ben's right boot shattered and he pitched backwards. Both barrels of the scattergun roared shot against the sky. Then McLain was running forwards, dropping the Sharps as he snatched the Dragoon clear of the holster. Ben was on his stomach, scrabbling for the fallen cartridges. McLain kicked him hard in the ribs. Then again in the belly. Ben screamed, twisting round. McLain went down on his knees, grabbing a fistful of shirtfront. He brought the Dragoon down and round in a vicious curve that ended along the side of Ben's jaw.

The pockmarked man grunted and went limp.

McLain stood up, toeing the scattergun away. Behind him, Sloane came out on to the sidewalk. He was trembling, wiping blood from his face. Spitting and gagging.

'String him up!' he yelled. 'Hang the bastard!'

'No!' McLain shook his head. 'I'm taking him back. I made a promise.'

And as he said it, he thought: Damn you, Janey Page.

Chapter Five

Early light woke him, filtering through the cracks in the roof. He opened his eyes, right hand tightening on the butt of the Dragoon as he turned on the narrow bed to stare at the man on the floor. Ben was tied wrists to ankles. A loop was fastened around his neck, running to McLain's left wrist. McLain unfastened it and tugged. Ben grunted and woke up. His eyes were bleary from the effects of the beating, but the glaze cleared fast, replaced by a look of pure hate.

McLain swung off the bed, wincing as the cuts along his ribs stretched.

Ben said, 'Christ! I'm dry.'

McLain ignored him, splashing water on his face and tugging his shirt into place. He pulled on his boots and ran his fingers through his thick hair. Then he loosed Ben's ropes enough that the man could stand up. Grabbed his shirtfront and hauled him upright. Ben grunted again.

'Move.' McLain gestured at the door. 'We're ridin' out.'

Ben grinned, his teeth unusually white.

'You ain't gonna make it, friend.'

'I'll make it.' McLain shoved him through the door. 'An' I ain't your friend.'

Ben went on grinning.

Inside the saloon Tod Sloane served them eggs and thick slabs of ham. McLain loosed the pockmarked man's wrists enough that he could eat. He noticed that Sloane kept well clear of Ben.

'What you know about him?' he asked.

Sloane shrugged. 'A drifter. Comes an' goes. Was mostly with the big feller.'

He shuddered at the memory.

Ben chuckled and said, 'Charley never did have much sense. Guess he saw that scattergun an' kinda lost his head.'

McLain stared at him, emptying his coffee mug.

'He said he's got friends. That right?'

'Some.' Sloane went on looking nervous. 'Drifters like him. They come an' they go. Might be best you got him out o' here.'

'Yeah.' McLain nodded. 'Soon as I get supplies.'

He stood up, dragging the cords around Ben's wrists tight. Then he yanked the man to his feet and propelled him out of the saloon. Schotter's Crossing was waking up, people peering from storefronts as McLain marched his prisoner down Main Street to the stable. No one spoke, but he was conscious of the eyes on his back and he had the unpleasant feeling that they weren't all friendly.

The old stablehand put a saddle on a pinto gelding while McLain stowed his gear on the grey. McLain helped Ben into the saddle and lashed his wrists to the horn. He fixed a length of rope under the pinto's belly, pinning Ben's ankles in place.

'You aimin' to do this every day?' asked the pockmarked man.

'Yeah.' McLain nodded. 'Less'n you try runnin' away.'

'Then what?' asked Ben.

McLain stared at him. 'Then I put a slug through your knee.'

There was a finality in his voice that drained the colour from Ben's face. He swallowed hard and said nothing more as the big Missouri man led the horses out into the sunlight.

McLain purchased supplies for the journey back to Garrison and mounted up. As he rode out the same eyes followed him. As they passed the saloon Ben called out, 'Be seein' you, Tod.'

Sloane went back inside the saloon and poured himself a measure of whiskey. He downed the glass in one fast swallow and poured another that he drank with equal speed. He was beginning to have second thoughts about helping McLain. Beginning to wonder why Ben Schuyler was so goddam confident.

What he had told McLain had been truthful. There had just been a few things left out.

Like the fact that Ben used Schotter's Crossing as a hide-out because the Texas Rangers had a five-hundred-dollar price on his head.

And that Charley Vareen had a brother.

And that Lowen Vareen was meaner than Charley and Ben put together.

He began to curse as he poured his third drink. It had been the thought of them raping and killing a twelve-year-old girl that had prompted him to back McLain. That and the idea he might cut himself in on the reward. But now the girl didn't seem to matter much, nor the money. What did matter was that Ben had been waiting for Lowen.

And Lowen Vareen might not take kindly to Tod's having a hand in the killing of his brother.

He was three-quarters through the bottle before he got his story worked out, and the final quarter gave him the confidence he needed to persuade himself he could tell it right. He kept that confidence bolstered up with more whiskey through the long, hot day and by the time Lowen rode in, he had it off pat. Even half-way believed it himself.

Two full days had passed before Lowen showed, and Tod Sloane was almost glad to see him: he was drinking his own profits away.

Lowen was fair as his brother, but where Charley had been big and muscular, Lowen was short and going to fat. His clothes were thick with trail dust, the fancy conchos decorating his pants dull beneath the greyish yellow coating. His small eyes scanned the room and settled on Sloane like a rattlesnake's.

'Where's Charley?'

Sloane was surprised that his voice sounded so even as he said, 'Dead, Lowen.'

Vareen grabbed a bottle and drank from the neck. He glared at the barkeep; waiting. Sloane poured himself a drink and composed his features into what he hoped was a tragic expression.

'Feller called McLain come through lookin' fer him an' Ben. Said somethin' about some trouble over to a place called Garrison.'

Vareen nodded. 'I know it. What trouble?'

'Somethin' about a girl.' Sloane wondered why the fat man wasn't showing more concern. 'McLain said they killed her. He said he was takin' them back. They tried to make a run, but he grabbed my shotgun an' downed Charley. Took his head clean off.'

'Law?' grunted Vareen.

'No.' Sloane shook his head. 'Not official. Didn't have no badge.'

'Was murder, then.' Vareen put the bottle down and reached for a glass. 'Ben?'

'McLain took him,' said Sloane. 'Rode him out hogtied to the saddle. Be travellin' slow, Lowen.'

'Yeah.' Vareen spat on the floor. 'How long ago?'

'Two days. I got Charley buried, Lowen. Put up a real nice marker.'

'Fuck Charley,' grunted Vareen. 'I told him to stay outta trouble.'

'You gonna let him go?' asked Sloane.

'No.' Vareen shook his head. 'I need Ben. What's McLain look like?'

Sloane described the big man. Vareen nodded. He made Sloane think of an undertaker listening to measurements for a coffin. When the barkeep had finished, Vareen asked for food. After that he took a whore and spent the remainder of the day and the whole of the night in her room. Then he climbed up on his horse and took off eastwards, following the way McLain had gone.

'How come you're doin' this?' Ben Schuyler stared at McLain across the fire. 'You ain't a lawman.'

'You killed the girl.' McLain wasn't sure why he bothered answering the man. Maybe it was a way of sorting out his own thoughts. 'I knew her.'

'Hell!' Ben shrugged under the blanket draped around his shoulders. 'That was Charley, not me. He was stupid. Kinda crazy. He didn't even know what he was doin'.'

'You did.' McLain fetched the silver necklace from his pocket. It glinted in the fire's light. 'You took this off her.'

'It was pretty.' Schuyler watched the big man speculatively. 'She didn't need it no more.'

'She was twelve years old.' McLain wondered what kind of animal he was talking to. 'She was just a child.'

'Looked older,' said Schuyler. 'Hell! I've had Mex whores been no more'n fourteen an' knew tricks'd curl yore toes.'

'She wasn't a whore,' rasped McLain. 'She was a kid you raped an' killed.'

Ben shook his head. 'Charley done it.'

'You was there,' said McLain, not believing him, 'you could've stopped him.'

'Not Charley.' Schuyler laughed softly. 'Not that dumb ox.'

'Tell that when they try you,' McLain grunted.

'Try me?' Ben looked surprised. 'Who the hell's gonna try me? There ain't no court o' law between here an' San Antone.'

'Be a court in Garrison,' said McLain. 'They'll try you there.'

'Sure,' said Ben. 'They'll be greasin' the rope now.'

McLain shrugged, not answering.

'Christ!' Schuyler spat into the fire. 'I don't understand

you. You ain't a bounty hunter, or you'd have killed me already. You ain't a lawman. What they payin' you?'

'Nothing,' said McLain. 'Not a thing.'

'Nothing?' Schuyler gaped. 'You crazy? What you doin' it for, then?'

'You wouldn't understand,' said McLain.

'I understand you're puttin' yore life on the line,' said Schuyler, his dark eyes getting foxy. 'Fer nothin'.'

'For something,' McLain corrected. 'Something you wouldn't understand.'

'Riddles.' Schuyler sneered. 'Goddam riddles. I'll tell you some plain facts, feller. We're ridin' into Comanche country, an' them bastards'll lift yore hair along with mine. No questions asked about who done what. That's a fact. Another is, I was waitin' around Schotter's Crossing fer a feller called Lowen Vareen. Now Lowen was Charley's brother an' he's meaner'n a tub full o' diamondbacks. He's gonna be comin' after you.'

McLain shrugged, still not speaking.

'That's two goddam facts,' said Schuyler, his voice getting softer; more persuasive. 'A third is, I could cut you in on somethin' real big. The reason me an' Charley was waitin' fer Lowen.'

He paused, watching McLain's face for some flicker of interest. When none showed, he continued:

'Fact is, we was plannin' a job. There's a Mex silver train goes by not far from Schotter's Crossing. Lowen's been watchin' it. Gettin' the time worked out right. It's a three-man job, an' with Charley dead we're gonna need someone good. I seen you use yore guns, so I know you're good. Might be I could talk Lowen into takin' you in. When he comes up on us.'

He stopped talking, staring at McLain's face with an expectant smile showing on his pockmarked features. McLain poured coffee. Drank it.

Schuyler said: 'Well? We reckon on liftin' around five

thousand dollars American. Split three ways, you'd be a rich man.'

McLain lifted the coffee pot. Spilled the grounds out.

'Shut yore goddam mouth.'

'Think about it,' urged Schuyler. 'That's a lotta money.'

McLain stood up. He grabbed the pockmarked man and drew the ropes around his wrists and ankles taut, forcing him to a kneeling position. Then he shoved Ben over and fastened a rope to his saddle.

'Ain't you interested?' Ben demanded. 'Beats gettin' killed.'

'You want me to gag you?'

McLain draped the blanket over the man's body as he spoke. Ben shook his head. He kept his mouth closed.

McLain spread his own blanket. The night was cold, a chilly wind blowing down from the north, rustling the trees so that the darkness was filled with a whispering sussuration like half-heard voices. The sky was clear, a deep velvet blue that was pricked through with the pinpoints of stars. The moon was waning, the round of the great yellow orb flattening out so that the craters pitting the surface gave it the appearance of a face peering knowingly at the world below. McLain watched it, letting random thoughts float through his mind.

It occured to him that he was working for nothing. What he made in Garrison hauling freight or scouting for the Army earned him no more than the bare necessities: he owned little more than he had ridden in with. Except he had a place to live and friends. Somewhere he belonged again. And that counted for a lot.

But if Garrison went on growing the way Alice planned, how long could he last? The town was expanding. Soon it would be a real town, with new people coming in and prices going up. One third of five thousand dollars was – he faltered, fetching up against the stumbling block of the calculation – around fifteen hundred, at least. More money than he had ever seen. More than he had ever thought of making.

He grunted, pushing the thought from his mind. What the hell would he do with that much money? The Rio Verde was cattle country and he didn't know a damn' thing about cows. Farming was what he knew – *had* known – but since the War he hadn't felt any urge to farm. A farm needed a woman on it, and there were too many memories there. Besides, who the hell would want to set up home with him? And who the hell was there, anyway?

Except, maybe, Janey Page.

The thought came unbidden into his mind. And with it came an image of the woman. And for the first time McLain recognised the feeling he had known only once before.

It was like a seed planted in the ground. Planted and forgotten, growing slowly, unnoticed, but all the time spreading, rooting, getting stronger. It wasn't yet ready to sprout, but it was there. And suddenly he knew exactly why he was chancing his life to bring Ben Schuyler in alive.

And again he cursed Janey Page.

Lowen Vareen had learnt his tracking skills riding with a bunch of Comancheros out of Chihuahua. He also had the advantage of knowing where his quarry was headed. Knowing, too, that his quarry had to be moving slower than him; maybe without realising he was coming up behind.

Those things gave him advantage enough to feel confident of catching up and freeing Ben Schuyler.

Charley was already a past issue in his mind. His younger brother never had amounted to much more than a pack of muscles and a fast gun: if he was stupid enough to get himself killed, then that was his problem. Not Lowen's. What made Lowen mad was the way this man called McLain had fouled up his plan. Lowen was topping forty as best he knew, not being sure of the exact date of his birth, and the raid on the Mexican silver train was to be his big strike. The one that would buy him freedom from running, from looking over his shoulder for Texas Rangers or *Federales* or peace officers. Freedom to make tracks for California, or maybe Mexico. Someplace he wasn't known where he could buy a spread or a whorehouse and sit back fat and rich on the proceeds. And to get the prize he needed at least one more man. Three would be best, but two could handle it if the other was someone he could rely on. Like Ben.

That was why he was determined to rescue Schuyler.

And soon. Before the silver train slipped by.

He rode hard through the first day, following the trail up into the hills without paying too much attention to sign. There was only one direct route through to the Rio Verde, and he figured McLain would go that way rather than chance any of the more circuitous trails. The way Lowen had it worked out, he would get ahead and lay up an ambush. Gun McLain and free Ben. Then a fast run back to Schotter's Crossing and wait for the silver train.

By the second day he was confident he was on the right track. He was moving faster and he had seen enough sign to be sure he was closing. He rode late into the night and started out before dawn the following day. By then he had McLain's lead cut down to a manageable distance and a clearer idea of where he could lay his ambush. There was a place about a day and a half ahead where the trail came over a ridge before dropping down into a slough of badlands that narrowed it down between walls of high stone. Approaching riders would be outlined against the sky, while a man down in the jumble of rock would be hidden in shadow.

Lowen Vareen turned his horse to steer off the trail, cutting north-east so as to overtake McLain and Schuyler.

Janey Page set her cup down and watched as Alice Docherty poured fresh coffee. Her fair hair was gathered back with a pale blue ribbon, emphasising the smooth planes of her face. Emphasising the creases worry set in twin lines between her eyes. She toyed with her cup, not really tasting the coffee she sipped with ladylike delicacy.

Alice drank hers with relish, then smoothed the folds of her pinafore neatly over her lean hips.

'What's on yore mind, Janey?'

The directness of the question caused the younger woman to smile, but when she spoke the worry lines were still there.

'Nothing, Alice. Really.'

'Nothing!' Alice snorted, pointing at the curtains they had spent the morning sewing. 'There's something troubling you – you been droppin' stitches faster'n a broody hen lays eggs.'

Janey smiled again, glancing at their handiwork.

'I'm sorry. I'll go over them again.'

'Don't worry about that.' Alice stared at her companion. 'It's John T., ain't it?'

It wasn't really a question and it brought a blush to the girl's face. She started to shake her head, but then the movement turned into a nod. A brief, almost curt, nod. Almost as though she was reluctant to admit it.

'He's been gone a long time.'

'Nine days.' Alice glanced at the grandfather clock set against the wall behind Janey. 'Nine and a half, counting today. Not that long.'

'But if he didn't know where they'd gone . . .' Janey let the words tail off.

'Man like John T.,' said Alice with supreme confidence, 'he's got ways of finding out. Besides, this is a big country, an' John T. don't give up easy.'

'Still.' Janey shrugged.

'Still he'll come back,' said Alice; firmly. 'An' how come you're so fretted up?'

'Oh, dammit!' Janey banged both fists on the table, threatening to spill coffee. 'I am worried about him. I don't know why, but I am.'

'Could be . . .' This time Alice let the words tail away. 'He can look after himself, Janey. You feel something for a man like John T., you can't let it fetter him. You could spend the rest of your life worrying about him.'

The blush on Janey's face got deeper. 'I don't know what you mean,' she said quickly. 'The rest of my life?'

Alice smiled fondly and shook her head. 'Maybe you know; maybe not. It can be funny, the way things happen.'

'If he has found them.' Janey spoke fast, seeking to cover her confusion. 'He promised to bring them back alive.'

'You talked him into that,' Alice remarked softly. 'You gettin' second thoughts?'

'I don't know.' Janey shrugged. 'That would be difficult, wouldn't it?'

'Don't reckon they'd come in easy,' Alice murmured. 'Be easier to kill them. Like they deserve.'

Janey stared at her. 'Is that how you'd have done it? Just shot them down?'

Now Alice frowned in confusion.

'Child,' she said slowly, 'you got a way with words as sometimes gets folk tied up. Back in the old days, before we had a town here, I'd have said yes and not thought twice about it. I'd have trusted John T. to find them an' kill them. An' I'd not have doubted he'd find the right ones. But we got us a town now, an' like you said: a town needs law. Without that, we ain't a proper town. Just one more settlement on the frontier, with the fastest gun bein' the one in the right. That means we need proper law. Not gunlaw. Means we need a man like John T. to uphold that law. But if he's gonna do that right, if we're gonna do things right, then it has to be all the way down the line.'

'But he could get killed,' said Janey. 'Two men against one.'

'He's handled worse odds,' said Alice; almost curtly. 'Besides, it's too late now. He'll come back or he won't. Simple as that.'

She set down her cup and picked up one of the curtains,

beginning to sew furiously. Janey watched her for a moment, then took her own needle and set to work.

After a while Alice said very quietly, 'He'll come back. He must come back.'

'Yes,' said Janey in the same quiet tone. 'Yes, he must.'

Lowen Vareen found the place he was looking for while the sun was still climbing towards noonday. The way he'd been riding he calculated on McLain coming over the ridge towards late afternoon. That meant the sun would be at his back, outlining him nicely against the sky: as clear a target as a man could wish for. He put his horse down in the shadowed cleft of a big overhang and gave it water from his canteen. Then he climbed up amongst the rocks until he found a spot that gave him cover and a clear line of fire. He began to chew on sour-dough biscuits and a chunk of salt pork, washing the food down with whiskey brought from Sloane's saloon.

He checked the load in the Colt's Army belted around his spreading waist and primed the Spencer repeating rifle, lowering the hammer carefully over the chamber. Then he eased his gut into a more comfortable position and tilted his curly-brimmed sombrero down over his face.

All he needed do now was wait.

Time passed, hot and slow. The sun beat down, then eased into afternoon. The shadows of the boulders lengthened. A gila monster watched Vareen from the top of a sunbaked rock. Vareen watched the gila: their faces had the same kind of indifferent menace.

More time went by. The gila moved. Vareen didn't.

The level of whiskey in the bottle went down in measure with the sun. Vareen wiped sweat from his face. The afternoon was very still. Very silent.

Silent enough that the steady clopping of hooves sounded clear on the bedrock of the trail.

Vareen corked the bottle and lifted the Spencer.

By the time the two men showed on the ridgetop he had

the rifle settled back tight against his shoulder, sighting down the long barrel with his forefinger snug on the trigger.

He recognised Ben Schuyler's pockmarked features and drifted his sights over to line the rifle on the chest of the big man in lead. He sucked in a deep breath and let it ease out slow as his finger closed the trigger and the Spencer kicked against his shoulder.

In the stillness the detonation was very loud.

Chapter Six

McLain heard the shot and started a sideways movement that would have shifted him clear of the saddle had he enough time.

Instead, the saddle seemed to shift under him and he felt his body crash against the hard ground. Pain lanced through his ribs and the world went black. He was dimly aware of the grey horse screaming and Ben Schuyler's whoop of pure glee, then his head was spinning too hard for him to be conscious of anything except pain and a great swirl of anger that came up from somewhere inside him and washed over his mind in waves of red.

Time became meaningless.

Pain became meaningless.

There was weight on him he knew he had to shift.

He spat blood and gritted his teeth, pushing against the weight.

He wasn't sure why he had to shift it. Knew only that he must.

The stone was hot under his palms. Hot as the waves of anger and agony flooding through his mind.

He went on pushing.

And the weight went away.

It went away so suddenly he jerked half-way upright, body twisting as instinct took over and fought to drag him to some kind of safety. Adrenaline coursed through his bloodstream, bringing with it that speeding of the metabolic rate that seems to slow external time. Seems to hurl the sufferer into action so rapid he is able to view the world around him at leisure.

McLain saw the grey horse down on its back with blood

still fountaining from the shattered frontage of its skull.

Saw Ben Schuyler driving the pinto down the ridge towards the jumble of broken stone where the shot must have come from.

Saw his own hand, bloody, reaching towards the Sharps scabbarded on his saddle.

Saw a flash brighten the shadows amongst the rocks.

Saw stone scar six inches from his face as a ricochet screamed through the suddenly noisy air.

Saw his hand close on the Sharps and drag the big carbine clear of the saddle.

There was a blur of motion as his body slowed and he rolled across the trail into the scatter of loose rock at the northern edge.

Chips blew in a cloud of dust and stinging fragments from the stone.

Once.

Twice.

A third time.

Oh Christ! McLain thought. He's got a goddam repeater.

A fourth shot. A fifth.

Then silence.

McLain realised the hidden shootist must be reloading. He risked a glance out round the scant cover. And saw Schuyler moving fast for the safety of the badlands.

He snatched the Sharps up to his shoulder, loosing off a shot that he hoped would hit right. Cursing the fact his hands were tied by promises and he couldn't just blow the pockmarked man out of the saddle into the hell where he belonged.

The pinto screamed. A long furrow of bright red blood showed on the left flank. The horse twisted on itself, bucking against the pain. Schuyler yelled something McLain couldn't hear, wobbling in the saddle as he fought to control the animal with lashed hands and tied feet.

His movements served only to panic the horse further. To

throw it off balance so that it went crashing over on its side with Schuyler screaming obscenities as he went down under the animal. Tied, he was unable to roll clear. And his bonds served to hamper the pinto as it fought to get back on its legs. It kicked helplessly, held down by Schuyler's weight as McLain thumbed a fresh charge into the Sharps. Capped the nipple. Crouched back behind the protective rock.

The repeater blasted again.

McLain counted the shots: seven. Then silence. He triggered the Sharps, sending a bullet blind into the shadowy stone below him.

There was a hoarse laugh, and a whiskey-throated voice bellowed, 'We got us a stand-off!'

McLain stayed silent.

The voice called again. 'I got you pinned down. Ain't no place you can run.'

McLain glanced round: the man was right. To his left there was a flank of rock high enough he'd need to stand up to cross it. Behind him, the ridge was bare. To his right, the trail was open. There was no place he could go.

He yelled, 'What you got in mind?'

'A trade,' shouted the hidden marksman. 'Yore life for Ben.'

McLain checked his body as he thought about an answer. His legs were bruised where the grey horse had rolled on him, and where he had hit ground his face and shoulder felt like he'd been kicked. His ribs were hurting, but there was nothing serious as best he could tell: the blood had come mostly from the horse, a little from his own cut lip. He wiped his hands down his pants, craning round to check the position of the sun: about three hours to dark.

'I'm takin' Ben in,' he called.

'You ain't takin' no one nowhere,' came the reply. 'You move an' you're dead.'

'Ben's dead,' McLain shouted, 'you try anything.'

'Like I said,' answered the hoarse voice, 'it's a stand-off. I want Ben, an' I guess you want to get out alive. You go down an' cut Ben loose, I'll hold fire. Let you walk home.'

'Thanks,' McLain grunted, guessing the shootist must be Lowen Vareen; not trusting him. 'Thanks for nothing.'

'Well?' Vareen called.

'No deal,' shouted McLain.

A volley of shots spanged off the rock, filling the warm air with dust and chips of flying stone. Vareen was good. McLain had to acknowledge that. He had chosen his spot well, not leaving McLain any place to run. Had he been using a single-shot weapon, the big Missouri man might have chanced a move, relying on his speed to get him to a better position from where he could work his way round the other's flank. As it was, the repeater could cut him down before he reached any kind of cover. Nor would darkness afford him much advantage: the waning moon was still shedding enough light that he would be clear on the trail if he tried to work down to get Ben. He could drift away, leaving Ben to Vareen. Or he could put a shot into the pockmarked man and end the stand-off that way.

Neither alternative suited his purpose. He had given his word that he would take Schuyler in alive: that was what he was going to do. Just how was something he needed to work out.

He settled back flat against the hot stone, waiting with dogged patience.

The afternoon dragged on towards sundown. From time to time they traded shots. Schuyler stopped yelling and the pinto gave up its attempts to regain its feet. Every so often the trapped man shouted for Lowen to come get him out and Vareen shouted back that he was doing just that. Twice, McLain tried a move, only to be sent back by Vareen's bullets. The shadows got a little longer. Slowly. Very slowly.

And then McLain saw something that was going to change the situation. Whether to his advantage or not, he didn't know. Knew only that it would change now. Dramatically.

Lowen Vareen was in amongst a tumble of boulders spread over a shelf that jutted out above one side of the trail. To his left, the shelf ended in a short drop; behind and to his right a wall of natural stone curved round, some twelve to fifteen feet high. On the edge of that wall McLain saw a face. It was a dark face, framed by long, dark hair. There were bands of paint on the face; three eagle feathers tipped with red woven into the hair. The face was peering down at Vareen's position.

A dark arm lifted briefly and the face disappeared. McLain let his eyes wander slowly over the rocks, gradually discerning shadowy bodies moving in the deeper shadows.

Then, a sudden blur of movement. The whistle of arrows, ending with the dull thudding of stone heads entering flesh. Vareen began to scream.

Lowen Vareen scarcely knew what hit him.

He was stretched out on the stone waiting for the big bastard up on the ridge to show himself long enough he could put a bullet in him, feeling confident it would happen sooner or later. Most likely come nightfall: McLain was obstinate enough he might risk showing himself in an attempt to reach Ben. His water and whatever food he was carrying was on the dead horse, and he didn't stand a hope in hell of reaching it without taking a slug. Vareen, meanwhile, was pretty comfortable. He had food and a canteen of untouched water. He was working his way down the second bottle of Sloane's whiskey. All he needed do was wait.

And then something dug into his back.

There was a moment of shock, as though a falling rock had hit him, replaced almost instantly by a searing pain that coursed like fire through his left shoulder, jerking his hand away from the Spencer. He gasped, twisting over on his side. And as he moved, there was a second blow, close to the first so that the two waves of pain ran together and he cried out loud.

He began to sit up, forgetting about McLain, glaring furiously into the shadows behind him. In time to see a painted face behind a bone bow that strummed like a Mexican guitar as the cord loosed the arrow. Vareen saw the arrow, first as a blur that sped towards his chest, then as a painted wood shaft with dark red feathers around the notched end that stuck out from his chest and threw him back.

He triggered a single shot. Heard it ricochet off the stone through the sound of his own screaming. Then he was doubling over as two more shafts hit his belly, the stone heads driving deep through the fat and the muscle. Deep into the softer stuff beneath.

He let go the rifle and clutched at the shafts, bunching them together in his big hands. He screamed afresh as they came loose, staring down at the red stain spreading over the front of his shirt. At the pieces of flesh and entrails hanging from the bloody tips.

He went on screaming as the Comanches closed in, staring up at the bright metal heads of the store-bought hatchets. He was still screaming as the first descended and sliced into his jaw, splintering bone and carving through the skin and tendons so that his face was split in two, the jawbone dangling loose on to his chest. His screaming changed then into a deep gargling sound that ended as another hatchet severed his throat and a third crashed against the base of his thick neck.

He never felt the cut of the Bowie knife that sliced his scalp and lifted his thinning yellow hair. Or the hands that tugged the gunbelt from his waist and ransacked his pockets for powder and ball.

McLain waited for the screaming to stop, hoping the Indians would be satisfied with whatever loot they found on Vareen.

He couldn't be sure how many there were, but the nature of the terrain meant that if they chose to attack him they would have to come from in front. He eased the Dragoon from his holster and rapidly primed the empty sixth chamber before setting the big pistol down on the rock.

Dusk was not far off now, but he knew the Comanches had no taboo about night-fighting. If the warriors wanted him, too, they would come in under cover of the darkness.

Then a voice that was oddly familiar called, '*Amigo!* You find man.'

'*Sí.*' He shouted back. 'Yes.'

Two braves showed. McLain recognised them as the leader of the group he had traded with and the spokesman. One held Vareen's Spencer, the other had the dead man's gunbelt draped over his shoulder. The leader said something, and the other laughed.

'Your axes cut good,' he called. 'Get us firesticks.'

Both Indians brandished their looted weapons.

'Horse, too,' announced the one who spoke English. 'Good horse. You keep other.'

'Yeah,' said McLain. 'Thanks. *Muy gracias.*'

'Good trade,' said the Indian. 'You go. Next time we kill you.'

McLain climbed to his feet. The Comanches faded back amongst the rocks and there was the sound of shod hooves mingled with the duller noise of the Indian ponies. He waited until he was sure they were gone, then took his gear from the grey horse and went down to where Ben Schuyler lay.

The pockmarked man was pale, fear draining the colour from his face so that the old scars stood out a fierce red. He watched in silence as McLain cut the pinto free and got the animal back on its feet.

When he spoke all his earlier confidence was gone: 'You got funny friends, mister.'

'Yeah.' McLain bent down to cut the man's feet free. 'But they got their points. Was them found you.'

‘Christ!’ Schuyler massaged his legs. ‘How’d you work that?’

‘Indian trading,’ grunted McLain. ‘Get up.’

He swung into the saddle. Schuyler moved towards the horse, lifting his tied hands in anticipation. McLain stared down at him, face cold.

‘Well?’ Schuyler asked. ‘You gonna help me up, or not?’

McLain shook his head. ‘You walk.’

The pockmarked man stared at him in disbelief. ‘You don’t mean that.’

‘Sure I do.’ McLain grinned. ‘Was your friend killed my horse. Mine left me this one.’

As they moved into the badlands a long spiral of buzzards came down through the darkening air, intent on using what daylight was left to pick over the corpse of Lowen Vareen.

Chapter Seven

'You could send out a patrol.'

Janey Page watched Frank Donnelly's face as she said it, looking for some hint of sympathy, some sign of compassion. There was none there, only a blank, impassive expression tinged with irritation.

'No,' he said. 'I'm sorry, Janey, but I can't do that.'

'Why not?' she demanded, trying to keep her own voice reasonable. 'You send patrols out all the time.'

'That's military business,' Donnelly answered. 'I have to maintain regular patrols.'

'But you've got men here,' she said. 'You could send them.'

'And suppose there was an attack?' he asked. 'Who's responsible for securing this outpost?'

'You, Frank.' She was almost wheedling now. Almost ashamed of it. Almost, but not quite. 'But surely you could . . .'

'No.' Donnelly's voice was firm: final. 'McLain went out of his own accord. He took that decision on himself – he has to answer any consequences.'

'He did it because the Koch girl was murdered.' Irritation was edging her voice now. 'He went looking for the killers.'

'And who gave him the authority?' snapped Donnelly. 'McLain is a private citizen. He's not a peace officer. No one asked him to go – that was his choice. If he wants to go roving over half Texas, I can't stop him. Nor can I act as wetnurse to every wandering saddletramp drifts into this place.'

'John McLain is not a saddletramp, Frank.' The irritation was clear now. 'He's the nearest thing this town has to a lawman. That's why he went after them.'

Donnelly snorted contemptuously. 'McLain may fancy himself some kind of peace officer,' he said, 'but that is pure assumption on his part. I represent the only legally appointed authority here. And I will not be bullied into employing the United States Cavalry to ride herd on a jumped-up Missouri guerrilla.'

Janey pursed her lips, not wanting to let her anger boil over.

'That's it, isn't it?' she said curtly. 'You resent him.'

'I assure you there is nothing personal in it.' Donnelly laughed, brushing at his moustache. 'I command the garrison here, and I cannot allow myself personal feelings.'

Janey nodded, the movement sarcastic.

'Perhaps you should, Frank. It might make you a little less pompous.'

Before Donnelly could answer she had spun round and was gone out the door. He watched it slam behind her and let a sigh ease from his lips. Why couldn't she see it, he wondered. Was she so besotted with McLain? Like every other damned civilian in the place? Things had to be done by the book. Without that, there was no authority. And without authority there could be none of that civilization she and Alice Docherty were always talking about. If they had their way, he might as well resign his commission and hand the place over to McLain. Let him protect them.

He took a cheroot from the box on his desk and struck a match. Sucking in smoke, he turned back to the report on hand. And a slow smile creased his handsome face: maybe McLain was in trouble. Maybe he wouldn't come back.

The smile got broader as the thought took hold; and outside, the trooper on guard duty wondered why Captain Donnelly was humming so cheerfully. It wasn't at all like the starch-back officer he had come to know and dislike.

Janey walked away from the cluster of buildings she thought

of as The Fort into the cluster she regarded as The Town. There was no clear dividing line, but somehow Garrison was this stretch of civilian structures out of Frank Donnelly's domain. The saloon and the attached store with Abe Kintyre checking over the hardware strung on display at the front; the clang of hammer on metal from Swede's smithy; Angus MacKay, gold spectacles glinting in the sun as he busily polished the glass fronting his barber shop-cum-funeral parlour; the livery stable down at the end of the single street, where One-Eye Peters was rocking lazily in the sun. Even the tents close by the barracks building, where Gomez kept his whores. The only other building was her own small shack. Built with the goodwill and hard work of the people who had adopted her as one of their own. Good people. Strong people. Like Alice and Shawn. Simple, straightforward frontier folk who were struggling to build something worth holding on to.

That was Garrison. And Garrison needed a man like John T. McLain. Needed his unofficial position made legal. Needed him appointed Peace Officer.

At least, she thought, his promise to bring Mary Koch's killers in alive was a step in the right direction. He hadn't made that promise easily, and she wasn't sure just what it was had prompted him. Maybe just a desire to quiet her arguments. Or maybe his own recognition of their sense. Whatever; that was logical thinking and right now she didn't feel very logical. What she felt was something she couldn't recognise because she had never felt it before, and so couldn't explain it to herself, or properly understand it. All she knew was that she hoped to God he would come back alive.

She climbed the steps to the saloon. Shawn Docherty was behind the bar, shirtsleeves rolled up over his brawny arms and collar open. He had a mug of beer in his hand and was deep in conversation with three soldiers.

They all looked up as she came in, and Shawn said: 'Janey, you've a face on you to sour milk.'

She smiled at him, unable to remain depressed under his good-natured beam.

'Where's Alice?' she asked.

'Out back.' Shawn pointed to the rear of the room. 'Fixing those curtains you been sewin'. Be glad to have someone other'n me to admire them.'

Janey nodded and went over to the door that opened into the Dochertys' private quarters. Like the other inhabitants – with the exception of herself – they lived where they worked. Originally there had been one medium-sized room built on to the saloon, but Shawn had taken it on himself to expand that, so now that room was a parlour and there was a bedroom and a proper kitchen added. There was a carpet covering most of the plank floor and a table with four straight-back chairs at the centre. Over to one side, spread around the fireplace there were three easy-chairs and an old wooden rocker. Alice was perched precariously on a stool, fixing the curtains in place.

'They look nice,' said Janey.

'They look civilized,' Alice remarked, climbing down to survey her handiwork. 'I spent long enough livin' with wood shutters with gunports cut in. You want to make us some coffee?'

'Sure.' Janey went through to the kitchen, calling back over her shoulder, 'I just spoke to Frank.'

'What's he got to say?' Alice asked.

'Not much.' Janey set the pot on the stove. 'I asked him if he'd send a patrol out. To look for John.'

Alice snorted. 'An' he said no. Right? I could've told you you'd be wastin' yore time.'

'It was worth trying.' Janey fetched cups from the big dresser. 'He said it was nothing to do with him.'

'He was right,' said Alice. 'It ain't. If it was Comanch' killed that poor little girl, then it'd be Frank's business. But it wasn't. It was white men, an' that makes it our business.'

Alice ruffled the curtains into place and went through to

help Janey bring the coffee in. The two women sat down at the table.

'It's like you said,' remarked the older woman. 'We got us a town now. A town that's growin' all the time. The way Frank sees things, we're just one more military outpost. But we know better. We know we got us a town, an' we know a town needs law. We can't leave that to the Army – we gotta handle that ourselves, an' that's what John T.'s doin'.'

'Is he?' murmured Janey. 'You really think he'll come back?'

'Sure,' said Alice. 'It ain't always the bad pennies keep turnin' up.'

'What if,' Janey started to say before correcting it to, '*When* he does? What do we do then?'

Alice frowned at her. 'Just what you suggested, miss. We hold a trial.'

'They'll find the men guilty,' said Janey. 'They'll vote to hang them.'

'Of course.' Alice smiled benignly. 'Be what they deserve. Better. But we'll have done it legal. We'll have shown Frank Donnelly that we run Garrison, not him.'

Janey shook her head. 'That's no better than lynch law, Alice. That's just putting a gloss on it.'

'What you expect?' asked the older woman. 'What you want, exactly?'

'The same as you.' Janey stared at her cup, trying to sort out her confused thoughts. 'A town. A *proper* town. With proper law. Not lynch law.'

'Girl,' said Alice gently, 'times are I think you got more learnin' than is good for you. How else can we do it?'

'I was thinking,' said Janey. 'We should send the men to San Antonio. There's a real court there. They could be tried legally. By the proper authorities. If – when – John brings them back, we should look at all the evidence and decide if they're really the ones who did it. Then we write it all down and send a report to San Antonio. We could ask for John to be made marshal at the same time.'

'They might not get far,' murmured Alice, thinking about it. 'Not the way folks round here feel about the killin'.'

'But we could talk to them.' Janey was warming to her subject now. 'Persuade them our way is right.'

'I ain't sure.' Alice sounded doubtful. 'I hadn't thought much beyond John T. bringin' them back.'

'We have to think further,' urged Janey. 'If Garrison is really going to be a proper town.'

'Yeah.' Alice swirled coffee around the bottom of her cup. 'Maybe you're right. Wouldn't be no problem gettin' John T. appointed, so long as he agrees. We'd just say the Garrison Citizens' Committee want him to be marshal, an' if Frank Donnelly objects I can send word to Nathan Cutler over to Fort Davis. He'll do what I ask. Then John T. delivers his prisoners an' they get hung in San Antone. John T. comes back with a badge an' we got us a proper lawman.'

She smiled at her own logic, then frowned again.

'There's just two problems.'

'What?' asked Janey.

'Gettin' John T. to agree an' gettin' them goddam murderers to the gallows,' said Alice. 'But we can work on those.'

'Yes,' nodded the girl. 'Yes, we can.'

And so McLain's future was decided for him. The process was not irrevocable, but it had behind it the dominating force of Alice Docherty's will and the sweetly calm persuasion of Janey Page. The one had got a town built chiefly through sheer determination and the other had earned a place of respect in the minds of Garrison's inhabitants. Together they made a team few people could safely argue against.

They set to work the same day. Alice explained their decision to Shawn and half-bullied, half-cajoled him into agreement. The saloon being the focus of social life in the settlement, they used it as a means of buttonholing, first the most important townsfolk, and then the others. Abe Kintyre – conscious of the Dochertys' share in his store – was easily persuaded. A trial of any kind would bring people in, and visitors bought goods. That was enough to satisfy Abe. Swede had a healthy respect for law and order, and agreed almost immediately that things should be done properly. Angus MacKay was persuaded with more difficulty: he had counted on providing the coffins and handling the burial arrangements, but he came round in the end. One-Eye Peters said he didn't care where the bastards were hung so long as he could feel sure they'd dangle. And Gomez just shrugged and told them to go ahead.

Frank Donnelly made noises about the authority of the military, but Janey reminded him that he had told her it was a civilian affair and Alice clinched it by suggesting she write a letter to Nathan Cutler. Donnelly was still aware that his refusal to listen to Alice and McLain had resulted in his prolonged posting – with the rank of captain – to the Rio Verde outpost and didn't deem it worth jeopardising his career any further.

After that it was easy. Gomez's whores did what they were told and MacKay's wife – a spindly little woman called Agnes – was afraid she'd be ostracized if she expressed her belief the men should be horsewhipped and then hung without trial. Johann and Inge Koch were still sunk too deep in grief to think beyond their loss and merely nodded dumbly when Shawn and Alice rode out to explain the plan.

The real problems came when the two women sat down to decide how the trial should be conducted.

'We can make up a jury all right,' Alice said, 'and Frank can be the judge. That'll make him feel he's got his precious authority still, an' bring the Army in.'

'Someone has to prosecute,' said Janey. 'And there has to be a defence.'

'You can handle that,' Alice said, a sly smile creasing her face. 'I'll prosecute the bastards.'

Janey went pale. 'Me? Why me?'

'Who else?' Alice countered. 'I don't see no one else agreein' to it. Besides, this was yore idea.'

'But I don't want to.' Janey shook her head. 'I can't.'

'You got the words, honey.' Alice's voice was sweetly reasonable. 'An' you're the one wanted it done legal. That means they gotta be defended. In the interests of the town.'

There was a logic to it that Janey couldn't deny. She tried arguing her way out, but Alice was implacable. In the end the younger woman was forced to agree.

'Fine,' said Alice. 'Now we got that all settled we just hafta wait for John T. to come back.'

He came back in the heat haze of a burning afternoon. Stubble decorated his cheeks and his eyes were hollowed from lack of sleep. He sat slumped in the saddle, trail dust greying his clothes and face.

The man he was leading at the end of his rope was in worse shape. His face was grey, as much from fear as from the dust, the grey pitted with a mess of ugly red smallpox scars. His eyes were dull and he tottered, limping on blistered feet that brought a groan of agony from his gaping mouth each time he took a step.

A crowd gathered as McLain rode up to the saloon, voices murmuring at first, but then lifting in anger. Donnelly came running from his command post with a squad of troopers and Shawn Docherty came out on the stoop, yelling for the crowd to stay back. McLain climbed down with the stiffness of a man with too much saddle time under him. Schuyler stood there as though too exhausted to make even the movement of collapsing. McLain passed the rope to Docherty.

'Name's Schuyler,' he grated through a mouth thick with dust. 'Ben Schuyler. The other got himself killed.'

'You?' Janey Page asked, staring at McLain.

The big man shook his head. 'No, ma'am. Not me. I done what I promised you, near as I could.'

He couldn't make up his mind if he was pleased to see her, or if the sight of her made him mad. He decided not to think about it. Not until he'd worked the kinks out of his body in a hot tub. A hot tub with a bottle of whiskey on the side. Then sleep. About twelve hours. After that he'd think about Janey Page.

'McLain,' she said as he climbed stiffly up the steps. 'John. I'm glad to see you back.'

'Yeah,' he answered.

And pushed past her into the saloon.

Chapter Eight

'Why me?'

McLain stared morosely into his glass, refusing to meet the eyes studying him intently from across the table. The saloon was shadowy, locked up for the night and lit by only a scatter of oil lamps. The pale yellow glow set an aura around Janey Page's fair hair, streaked Alice's grey with silver, transformed Shawn's stubble to a white frizz. A moth beat its wings silently against the glass funnel of one lamp, intent on destroying itself in the flame. Shawn reached across to pour more whiskey.

'Who else?' murmured Alice. 'You're the only one, John T.'

'She's right,' said her husband. 'There ain't no one else we could trust.'

McLain raised his glass, the movement lifting his eyes so that they met Janey's. She was staring at him, not saying anything. McLain was grateful for that: she could tie him up with words and have him tripping over his own tongue before he knew what he was saying. What he was agreeing to. And this was something he needed to think about.

'I need time,' he said. 'To think it out.'

'We don't have time,' said Alice. 'Right now we got folks persuaded we should do this right, but that ain't gonna last while that murderin' bastard sits in Frank's lock-up. There's some already sayin' as how we should string him up an' have done with it. We wait, they'll take him out an' lynch him.'

McLain grinned: 'Might not be a bad idea.'

Janey spoke then, her voice soft; persuasive.

'You rode a long way to bring him back, John. You risked

your own life to bring him back alive. Do you want to throw all that away?'

'He's gonna hang anyway,' grunted McLain. 'What difference does it make where?'

'None to him,' replied Alice, picking up the argument. 'But a whole lot to us.'

'I don't see it.' McLain frowned. Swallowed whiskey. 'What difference?'

'You remember when you come here?' asked the grey-haired woman, eyes crinkling in a fond smile. 'How we talked about gettin' a town started? A real town?'

'Sure.' McLain nodded, answering the smile. 'An' now you got that. You can hang him in a real town.'

'No.' Alice shook her head, the smile replaced with the earnest expression McLain recognised. 'A real town's got a real marshal. Real law. Not lynch law.'

McLain thought he recognised the thinking of Janey Page in there somewhere. He glanced at the girl, but she was just sitting with her face grave, hands clasping her coffee cup. It occurred to him that he had never seen her take a drink. Occurred, too, that she had very delicate hands, long-fingered and soft looking. The kind of hands that would feel good on a man's body.

Alice pressed her point: 'That means we got to do it legal, an' we can't do that without we get the authority from San Antone. You take him in there an' explain things to the judge, then he gets hung an' you come back with a badge.'

'Wouldn't be doin' no more'n you do already,' said Shawn. 'Exceptin' o' course you'd start gettin' paid for it.'

'I don't know.' McLain shrugged. 'I never figgered to be no lawman.'

'Hell!' said Shawn. 'You're near as dammit that, anyways.'

'An' we don't have no one else,' said Alice.

She was right, and McLain knew it. All their arguments held an implacable logic that he could no more deny than he could halt the flow of the river coursing down the valley. He hadn't looked for it, but he was the only man in Garrison with the standing or the physical authority to handle the job. The others all had vested interests, or were too old to handle it, or too young, or too quick-tempered. He looked again at Janey Page.

'What you think?' He paused a moment before adding, 'Janey.'

She looked at him with surprise registering on her pretty features, knowing she had to choose her words carefully.

'We need law,' she said. 'A town needs law the same way it needs people. Without, it's just a place. The more people come here, the more we'll need a peace officer. Someone to settle all the arguments. Someone to look after the town.'

'You could hire someone,' he muttered. 'A better gun than me.'

'We don't need a gun,' she answered, eyes fastened on his. 'We need a man. Someone we know. Someone people trust because they know he's fair. Straight. Someone people respect.'

'But why San Antone?' he asked. 'Why bother with that?'

'Because that's how the law works,' said Janey. 'We hang Schuyler here, then we're no better than a lynch mob. We'd just be prettying it up.'

'But he'll hang anyway,' argued McLain. 'Here or San Antone.'

'But no one could say we took the law into our own hands,' she replied. 'He'd be condemned by a proper judge.'

'All right.' McLain nodded. 'I'll take him to San Antone. That still don't mean I have to be a lawman.'

'You agree we need one?' Janey asked.

McLain nodded again: 'I guess.'

'And you must admit you're the best man for the job?'

'Of course he is,' smiled Alice. 'There ain't no one else.'

Janey flashed a brief smile in the direction of the older woman, then turned back to McLain: 'A man with a badge has authority. You'd hold a legal appointment that no one could argue with. Even new people coming in – they couldn't say you were just some local man with a gun. You'd have the badge from San Antonio.'

She stopped, staring at him intently. McLain stared back. Then at Alice. At Shawn.

'You really want this? You really want me to say I'll do it?'

'We ain't been talkin' about nothin' else,' smiled Alice, sensing a victory. 'Of course we want you.'

Shawn nodded, grinning.

McLain looked at his glass. Slowly he reached out for the bottle. Poured himself a measure. He held the glass a long time, unable to think of any other arguments to combat their logic. He felt proud of the trust they placed in him; felt more than ever that he belonged here. That he had a place somewhere again.

'How about the others?' he asked cautiously, still looking at the glass. 'Swede an' Abe an' the rest? What do they think?'

'Same as us,' Alice declared. 'They want it, too.'

McLain lifted the glass. 'All right. I'll go along.'

He drank, hoping he had made the right decision as Shawn whooped a great bellow of pure glee and Alice sniffed a tear, dabbing at her eyes. Janey Page smiled and reached out to touch his hand.

'Thank you, John,' she said.

Her touch was as soft as he had expected.

The trial was scheduled to take place in two days' time. Randall French came in from his spread with four hands he told McLain were at his disposal any time he needed them. Settlers from the outlying homesteads began to arrive and Garrison took on a circus atmosphere. On McLain's suggestion, weapons were checked in with Shawn and locked in a back room, guarded by one of Donnelly's men.

The Kochs arrived, Inge wearing a black dress with a black shawl covering her hair, Johann looking uncomfortable in a black suit new-bought from Abe Kintyre. Alice invited them both into her parlour and McLain followed.

'You found them.' Inge's voice was dull. 'The men who killed my little girl.'

'Yeah.' McLain nodded, not sure what to say. Uncertain how to say it right. 'There were two. I brought one in. The other got his head blowed off.'

'Good.' Under the shawl, Inge's mouth creased in something like a smile. '*Ist gut.*'

McLain pointed at the Colt's Navy stuck in Johann's belt. 'Have to ask you for that, Johann.'

The German stared at him, eyes blank and red-rimmed.

'I give you the gun when you give me your word.' His accent combined with his grief to make his voice guttural. 'The man must die, John. You promise me that before I give you my gun.'

'I got appointed marshal,' said McLain. 'I can't make you no promise like that.'

Christ! he thought, I'm sounding like a regular lawman now. He looked to Alice for help.

She said: 'We have to try him, Johann. Don't see there'll be much doubt about the outcome. The bastard'll hang. But in San Antonio. John T.'ll take him there after we tried him.'

Koch licked his lips. 'He will die?'

'Sure,' said Alice. 'He'll die.'

'*Gut.*' Koch took the pistol from his belt like a man unfamiliar with the weapon. 'Then I give you my gun.'

'Thanks.' McLain took the Colt and thrust it in his own belt. 'I'm sorry.'

'*Ja.*' Koch nodded. 'You will make a good marshal, John.'

McLain ducked his head and quit the room. There was too much grief there: he hoped keeping the peace wasn't always going to be like this. He stowed the pistol with the others and went out into the saloon. The room was crowded, the tables shifted back close against a wall and the chairs lined in rows. Smoke filled the air along with the babble of voices and there was a lot of drinking going on. It reminded him of the excitement preceding the appearance of the DeVere troupe, the night the Kochs had come in with Mary's body.

He nodded to Shawn and went out, pacing down Main Street to Donnelly's cabin.

The trooper on guard nodded and opened the door. Donnelly was behind his desk, wearing his dress uniform for the occasion.

'Well, McLain,' he said, a smile that was not quite a sneer decorating his mouth, 'you've come a long way.'

'For a Johnny Reb?' asked McLain, evenly.

Donnelly shrugged, not replying.

'You want to bring him over, Frank?' The big man kept his voice calm. 'Or shall I fetch him?'

'Perhaps we should both do it.' Donnelly stood up, brushing his uniform straight. 'We appear to hold equal authority now.'

'Best we get that straight,' said McLain. 'You run yore soldiers, I'll run the town.'

Donnelly's face got red. There were some things about being a lawman, McLain thought, that made the job worthwhile. He watched as Donnelly went to the door and barked orders, waiting as a squad of troopers brought Ben Schuyler out. The man had shackles on his wrists, but something of his old confidence had returned. He glared at McLain and spat into the dust.

'He told me something interesting,' murmured Donnelly. 'Something about Comanches letting you go free because you'd traded with them. I shall have to report that, of course.'

'You do that,' grunted the Missouri man. 'You report away, Frank. At least I brought him in.'

Donnelly glowered at him, his expression not much

different to Schuyler's. He settled his kepi neatly on his trimmed hair and waved a sarcastic gesture in the direction of the saloon.

'Shall we go? *Marshal*.'

McLain grinned, enjoying the officer's irritation, and led the way down the street without waiting to see if Donnelly was following.

The saloon went quiet as they entered. Donnelly positioned his men around the prisoner – a lynching would not look good on his career summary. Ben Schuyler was seated to one side of the tables, two husky privates standing either side. Donnelly assumed the central position with Alice and Janey seated to left and right.

'Very well,' he announced, pitching his voice as though on the parade ground, 'the court is now in sitting. Anyone making trouble gets ejected. The prosecution will proceed.'

Alice stood up and outlined what McLain had found up at the Koch place. She called on McLain to describe finding Schuyler and Charley Vareen in Schotter's Crossing, taking care to leave out the exact method he had used to trail them. She told the room how Schuyler had confessed to the murder, and then called on Johann Koch to identify the necklace McLain had found on the prisoner's wrist. McLain himself was called to describe Schuyler's confession.

From the back of the room someone called, 'Why we wastin' time? He's guilty as hell.'

Donnelly banged on the table and called for order.

Janey Page stood up with her face pale, an expression of distaste pursing her mouth.

'Do you deny killing Mary Koch?' she asked.

'Yeah.' Schuyler glanced round the room. 'Was Charley done it. Like I told McLain.'

'You had no hand in it?'

Schuyler shook his head, assuming an aggrieved expression. 'I tried to stop him. I couldn't on account o' Charley was a big feller an' kinda crazy. He just went mad.'

There were a few more questions, then both women summed up. Alice rested her case on the facts that John T. McLain was the best goddam tracker in the territory and if he said he'd trailed the two men to Schotter's Crossing then they were guilty; Schuyler was found wearing Mary's necklace on his wrist; and he'd told McLain he'd raped the girl; besides, he wore a gun and even if his partner was a big crazy man, he could have shot him to save Mary. Janey pleaded circumstantial evidence without much conviction, saying that Schuyler had been too frightened of Charley to risk shooting him, and just because he'd been there didn't make him a rapist or a murderer.

It was – to all intents and purposes – a travesty. The conclusion was foregone, and it took the jury exactly forty seconds to raise their hands and pronounce Ben Schuyler guilty as hell. What it did achieve was the acceptance of some kind of law in Garrison beyond mob justice. Beyond lynch law. It served to show the townsfolk and the settlers that they couldn't take the law into their own hands.

Donnelly pronounced the 'official' verdict: that a report should be prepared to be delivered – together with the prisoner – to the court in San Antonio, where he had no doubt that Ben Schuyler would be hanged by the neck until he was dead.

They got Schuyler out of the saloon fast. Before the audience got a chance to turn ugly and string the man up. Shawn bellowed that the first round was on the house – to celebrate the coming of law to Garrison – and the serious drinking began.

'You'd best get him out fast,' said Donnelly after they had Schuyler safely locked away. 'The novelty will wear off soon.'

'Yeah.' McLain had to acknowledge the sense of it. 'I'll take him out soon as that report's ready.'

'You think you can make it?' asked Donnelly. 'There'll be people travelling the same way.'

'Randall French an' his boys'll ride as far as the Seven,' answered McLain. 'After that I reckon I can handle it on my own.'

'I wonder,' murmured Donnelly. 'I wonder if you can guard him that far.'

'Hell, Frank,' McLain grinned. 'That's what a marshal does, isn't it?'

Chapter Nine

McLain got a chance to test his new authority sooner than he'd expected.

He left Frank Donnelly working on a report, and went over to Janey's cabin. Since they'd finished the structure and the newly-widowed woman had thrown a party to celebrate, he hadn't been inside the place. Now he tapped on the door feeling oddly nervous. He was a straightforward man, accustomed to seeing things plain and dealing with them the same way. Somehow Janey Page had a habit of wrong-footing him, and for a long time their relationship – such as it was – had been prickly, like two people with feelings for one another they were reluctant to recognise and so covered up with argument. To McLain's plain-speaking Missouri mind Janey was a mite too Eastern genteel, too much concerned with the niceties of things and maybe blind to the harsh realities of life on the frontier. He had always assumed that she saw him as a roughneck; one more wild westerner who used his guns instead of his brains. Yet since he had brought Ben Schuyler in, her attitude appeared to have changed, to have softened. And that left McLain as confused about her as ever.

He took off his hat as she opened the door. She was wearing the blue dress she had on for the trial, but now the cuffs were folded back and there was a smudge of ink on her right hand.

'John!' She sounded surprised to see him. 'Come in. I was just writing up the report.'

'I ain't disturbin' you?'

She smiled, shaking her head, stepping aside to motion him into the little room.

It was plain, but still comfortable. Feminine without being fussy. The floor and walls and ceiling were plain wood, scrupulously cleansed, with a rectangle of carpet at the centre where a small table was littered with paper and an inkpot. The windows were curtained in bright blue gingham, and the same material covered the two easy-chairs set either side of the stone fireplace. A couple of pictures decorated one wall, one depicting a woodland scene with a deer peering out from amongst the trees, the other a half-length portrait of a mustachioed man with a silver beard and features that reminded McLain of the woman.

'My father,' she explained. 'I managed to rescue it from the wagon.'

McLain noticed that she made no reference to her dead husband. She never spoke of *our* wagon, or *our* home. It was as though the man had been expunged from her memory. As though she had chosen to make a completely fresh start in Garrison.

'Coffee?' she asked. 'Please sit down.'

McLain nodded, easing into a chair as she went through to the tiny kitchen and began to bustle about with cups and a coffee pot. The room smelled clean and somehow of her. It wasn't scent, nor any particularly female smell; just fresh. It reminded him of his own farm.

'I was wonderin' how long it'd take you,' he said when she brought the coffee in. 'The report, I mean.'

'Are you in a hurry to leave?' she smiled, taking the other chair. 'You only just got back.'

'It ain't that.' He shrugged, taking the cup she offered him. 'Fact is, I don't like puttin' temptation in front of folks.'

'What do you mean?' Janey proffered sugar in a silver bowl. 'Temptation?'

'Schuyler's been found guilty,' he said. 'Right now folks are willing to go along with what you an' Alice cooked up. See him taken off to San Antone. But they know what he done an' they know he's in Frank's lock-up. Time they've drunk enough whiskey, they'll start wonderin' why we're botherin' to send him all that way to get hung when they could do it themselves. It's gonna be an awful temptation to lynch him.'

'Frank has men,' she murmured, looking at him with an expression of surprise and respect on her pretty face. 'He'll guard him, won't he?'

'Sure he will,' said McLain. 'It wouldn't look good on his record if he let a prisoner get taken from him. But that could just make things worse.'

'How so?' she frowned.

'The best intentions in the world get lost when a man's been drinkin',' said McLain. 'An' if there's a few hotheads to get them fired up, there could be a lynch mob goin' up against Frank's soldiers. That could get ugly. Sooner I can take Schuyler out, the less likely that is to happen.'

'John!' Now the respect was showing in her voice. 'You really take your new job seriously, don't you?'

McLain shrugged, feeling embarrassed.

'If I'm gonna do it, I'll do it the best I can. I don't want to start with a riot.'

'You're right,' she murmured. 'Of course. I've been trying to get the words just right, and I'd not thought of that.'

'Sooner you get them right, the sooner I can take him out,' he remarked. 'Why I asked you how long.'

'First thing in the morning.' She said it firmly. 'I'll have it written up for everyone to sign.'

'Everyone?' McLain asked.

'Alice and Shawn; Frank,' she nodded. 'Swede and Abe. All the leading townsfolk. That way it really looks official.'

'Yeah.' McLain allowed her to refill his cup. Helped himself to sugar. 'A death warrant.'

'You disapprove?' She looked at him with a curious expression.

'Hell, no.' McLain shook his head. 'Just seems like the law's an awful complicated thing.'

‘I suppose it is,’ said Janey. ‘That’s why we need someone like you to handle it here.’

McLain was about to reply when there was a pounding on the door. He rose to his feet, watching as the woman crossed the room. The door opened on Swede. His ruddy face was creased up; nervous. He was running a hand over the short white stubble covering his squarish skull.

‘Janey?’ His voice was anxious. ‘Thought I might find John here.’

‘You did,’ McLain said. ‘What’s wrong?’

Swede came into the room, Scandinavian propriety causing him to scuff his boots at the entrance.

‘There’s trouble, John.’ Anxiety thickened his accent, emphasising the lilt. ‘A mob forming.’

McLain glanced at Janey.

‘You were right,’ she said. ‘I’ll come with you.’

‘No.’ He settled his stetson on his thick hair. ‘You stay right here. Get that paperwork done.’

His tone was firm, commanding: it was an order.

Janey said, ‘You can’t tell me what to do, John T. McLain.’

He grinned at her, pausing in the doorway. ‘You made me marshal, right? That has to mean I *can* tell you what to do. Swede’ll stay with you.’

‘Why?’ she asked. ‘No one will hurt me.’

‘You was defendin’ Schuyler,’ grunted McLain. ‘They might not like that.’

He pushed past the brawny Scandinavian into the warm twilight air.

‘Keep the door locked, Swede. Stay with her.’

‘*Ya*, John. I do that.’

Janey glared at the closing door, mouth open in outrage. Then she smiled, shaking her head as she began to chuckle.

‘What is so funny?’ asked Swede.

‘Me,’ she said. ‘Him. I’m arguing with myself.’

Swede stared at her, his face puzzled.

'John will handle it,' he said firmly. 'He will be a good peacemaker.'

'Yes,' said Janey. 'Yes, he will.'

McLain went down the street at a lope. He was wearing his good suit – his one suit – in honour of the solemn occasion of the trial, and as he reached the saloon he pushed the tail back over the butt of the Dragoon holstered on his right hip. He hoped he wouldn't need to use the gun. Preferably not at all, but at least not the business end. He went up the steps at a run, crashing in through the batwings with his hand close to the pistol. Shawn Docherty looked across from behind the bar.

'Swede said there was trouble,' McLain grated, keeping his voice low enough that only Shawn could hear. 'Where?'

'Out back.' Shawn answered in the same low voice. 'Some o' the homesteaders got it in their heads we was wastin' time.'

Randall French came over, his walking stick clicking on the plank floor. Behind him, his cowboys watched like men waiting for a signal.

'John?' French nodded briefly. 'Say the word and you've got my boys to back you.'

'No.' McLain shook his head. 'Best you stay outta this, Randall. We get homesteaders an' French Seven men tradin' shots there'll be more trouble than we got already.'

French looked disappointed. 'Whatever you say. But the offer stands.'

'Thanks.' McLain smiled briefly. 'But stay put in here.'

'You want this?' Shawn set the cut-down scattergun he kept under the bar in McLain's reach. 'Best crowd stopper I know.'

'Don't reckon so.' The big Missouri man grinned ruefully. 'I can't handle this on my own, I reckon you made the wrong man marshal.'

'Whatever you say.' Shawn looked doubtful. 'But you better move fast. Them boys been hittin' it hard.'

'Yeah.' McLain turned away. 'Where're the Kochs?'

'With Alice,' said Shawn. 'In back.'

'Keep them there.' McLain crossed to the door. 'Keep everyone in here.'

'You got it.' Shawn watched him go out into the dusk.

He went down the steps and circled round the building at a run. Behind the saloon, the corral and outbuildings were silent, empty save for the horses. There was a litter of empty bottles glinting in the waning moonlight, and a few cigarette stubs still glowing on the packed dirt.

Further down, between the outlines of the barber shop and the Army store sheds, there was a dark, amorphous mass moving towards the solitary building that served Frank Donnelly as a jail. Voices were raised drunkenly, chanting something that sounded like 'Bring him out. String him up.' McLain decided that if they were going to do things properly, they'd need to build a civilian jailhouse. He ran back past the saloon and hurried down Main Street, getting ahead of the crowd.

Outside the lock-up two troopers were holding rifles braced across their chests. Both guns had long, ugly-looking bayonets fixed.

'Get outta here.' McLain came out of the shadows. 'Go tell Donnelly to stay put.'

'I don't know.' The older of the two troopers glanced from McLain to the approaching mob. 'We got orders from the Captain.'

'I'm countermandin' them.' McLain put a note of fierce authority into his voice. 'Don't get mixed up in civilian trouble.'

The soldiers glanced at one another. Then the older one shrugged and said, 'Hell! Why not?' and they took off in the direction of Donnelly's command hut. McLain stepped in front of the door. The lock-up was built of adobe taken from the ruins of the old Spanish Mission, solid blocks of ancient stone with a thick tiled roof. The door was heavy timber, with a big metal lock, and the small, square windows were barred.

From inside, Ben Schuyler yelled, 'What the hell's goin' on?'

'Lynch mob,' McLain answered. 'Got a yen to see you hang here.'

'You're the goddam lawman,' called Schuyler. 'You do yore goddam duty.'

'What I reckon on, feller,' grunted McLain.

And stepped out to face the mob.

There were around seven men, all of them drunk. Most were newcomers, either total strangers or barely known to McLain. The only one he recognised was a big, red-faced man called Hansen. He seemed to be the leader.

'All right!' McLain's voice halted them. 'What you want?'

'What the hell you think?' Hansen was swaying slightly, a half-empty bottle in his left hand. 'That goddam killer.'

McLain looked at him, checking the Dragoon holstered on his waist. Hansen had his hand close to the gun, but he wasn't touching it yet. The others carried an assortment of weapons, some wearing pistols, a couple holding shotguns. McLain felt the same way he had waiting for the Comanches to ride in.

'He's goin' to San Antone,' he said evenly. 'To get hung there.'

Hansen laughed, spittle spraying from his fleshy lips.

'Long way off, San Antone. He could get away.'

'Not from me.' McLain kept his eyes moving over the men, watching for a move. 'I brought him in. I'll get him there.'

'No point to wastin' time,' rasped Hansen. 'We'll do the job here. Now.'

'No you won't.' McLain decided they wouldn't try anything without the red-faced man's lead. 'We do this legal.'

‘Be legal,’ Hansen snarled. ‘He’s been tried. Bastard’s guilty. We want to see him swing.’

‘Ride to San Antone,’ snapped McLain. ‘Watch it there.’

‘Too goddam far.’ Hansen’s voice was whiskey-thick. ‘Do it here.’

‘Go back!’ McLain’s voice was a whiplash crack now. ‘Don’t make trouble for yoreselves.’

‘Ain’t makin’ trouble,’ grunted Hansen. ‘Makin’ a hangin’ party.’

He laughed at his own joke, the sound picked up by his followers. McLain decided to take him out fast and first. If it came to that. He hoped it wouldn’t. Hoped he could reason with them. The thought of the two scatterguns was an unpleasant itch that seemed to centre in the pit of his stomach, reminding him of Charley Vareen’s skull exploding.

‘The Kochs,’ he said so they could all hear him, ‘they ain’t no part of this. They want to see it done legal. You figger you got a better claim than them?’

Someone said, ‘Christ! I never thought of that.’

Someone else said, ‘He’s right, Hansen.’

The red-faced man ignored them. He glowered at McLain from eyes made pink and pig-like with the effects of the liquor.

‘I want to see it done here,’ he snarled. ‘Right here an’ right now.’

‘Don’t make me draw on you.’ Now McLain addressed himself directly to the big man. ‘Don’t get yourself hurt.’

‘Shit!’ Hansen took a step forwards, hand touching his pistol now. ‘You ain’t even a proper marshal. You can’t tell me what to do.’

He let the whiskey bottle go as he said it. The glass thudded on the dirt, not breaking, but sending a column of liquor fountaining over his dusty boots. The Dragoon came out of the holster and he took another step towards McLain.

The Missouri man moved fast, wanting now to get it done.

Get it finished before the two with the scatterguns made up their minds to join in. He closed the distance between them in a single long stride, left hand reaching out to grab Hansen's right wrist. The homesteader was as tall as McLain and about the same build. What he lacked in speed, he made up for in brute strength: it was hard to hold his gunhand down.

McLain twisted the wrist, forcing it out to the side as he snatched his own gun clear of the holster in a single fluid movement. The mob gasped, anticipating the gunshot, not certain what to do; not wanting to risk shooting the leader. McLain brought his gun up in a sweeping sideways motion, right arm flinging out to full length. Then he swung it in, laying the length of the barrel along the side of Hansen's skull.

The red-faced man grunted. His eyes opened wide and glazed. Then closed. His knees started to buckle. McLain hit him again, the blow opening an ugly welt along his temple. The Dragoon fell from his fingers and he followed it down into the dust, measuring his length on the ground.

McLain stepped back, Colt levelled from the waist.

'Now pick him up an' get the hell outta here!'

Two men came forwards sheepishly. They grabbed Hansen under the arms and began to drag him away. The others faded into the shadows. McLain let a long, slow sigh whisper from between his clenched teeth, waiting until they were all dispersed before holstering the Dragoon.

'You handled that well.'

McLain turned at the sound of Donnelly's voice.

'Were you watching?' He didn't know whether he should be angry, or not. 'All the time?'

'Sure.' Donnelly smiled. 'I didn't like to interfere in a civilian matter.'

McLain went on staring at him, anger and relief mingled in his expression.

Donnelly went on smiling. 'I just did what you asked,' he said evenly. 'Marshal.'

This time there was no sarcasm in his voice.

Chapter Ten

Morning dawned hot and golden. Mist steamed from the canebrakes along the banks of the river, swirled by the warm wind blowing in from the east. The sky was a clear, near-silver blue, flecked with the high-up shapes of drifting white cloud. Birds sang along the river, and overhead a skein of geese arrowed northwards. Smoke rose lazily from the chimneys of the town, caught by the wind and carried off towards the distant bulk of the hills. There was a smell of coffee and bacon and frying eggs. Horses snickered down amongst the Army hutments, answered by the mounts in the corral behind the saloon and by those penned outside the livery stable. A bugle clarioned in the still air, followed by the shout of orders and the stamp of feet as a squad of troopers swung into drill practice.

McLain scraped a razor over his cheeks and pulled on a fresh-laundered shirt. The cotton smelled clean and fresh: homely, like the sounds and the sights coming in through the window of his room. He buckled his gunbelt around his waist and went outside to the corral. The bay gelding whinnied a greeting, and he ran his hand over the velvety muzzle, murmuring softly to the big horse.

Back inside the saloon Alice set a plate of food before him and filled a tin mug with coffee. For no particular reason he remembered the delicate china cups Janey Page had used.

'You did good last night.' The grey-haired woman set a hand on his shoulder as she spoke. 'You handled it real well.'

'Just doin' my job,' McLain grinned.

'I guess.' A troubled look passed over her face. 'I never figgered on a lynch mob, though.'

'It happens,' he mumbled through a mouthful of eggs. 'Set

me to thinkin'. Be best we built our own jailhouse, sooner than use Frank's.'

'That'd make a difference?'

'I think so.' McLain nodded. 'Make it more official. Besides, it'd keep the Army out of things.'

Alice shrugged her agreement and bustled off to the kitchen as Randall French came in with his men. The latest addition to the saloon was a single long room with bunks, where travellers could spend the night. French joined McLain and helped himself to coffee.

'You'll be riding with us as far as the ranch?' he asked.

'Yeah.' McLain smiled. 'That should be far enough to lose any more like Hansen.'

French stroked his moustache, lean features creased in a smile.

'I saw him leaving. Nursing his head in the back of a wagon.'

'Could be a lesson there,' said McLain. 'Maybe next time we hold a trial we should stop sellin' liquor.'

'You want to do me out of business?' Shawn Docherty came in, cheeks shining pink from the application of a razor.

McLain shook his head, thinking that marshalling was going to produce a whole lot of problems he hadn't thought about before. Whatever they had said when they persuaded him to accept the job, pinning a badge on him was going to change the situation in Garrison in ways no one had thought out all the way.

'No,' he murmured. 'But we'll need do something to stop folk like Hansen tryin' to take the law in their own hands.'

'The badge should help,' grinned Shawn.

'And the man behind it,' added French.

Janey Page came in then, clutching a sheaf of neatly-lettered papers.

'It's all done,' she said. 'I've written it all up, and asked the judge to appoint John our marshal.'

She set the papers down on an empty table and offered the

pen to Shawn. He took it with exaggerated caution and inked his name laboriously in the place the girl indicated. Randall French signed, and then Alice.

'That's everyone except Frank,' said Janey.

McLain pushed his plate away and stood up.

'Let's get his name now. Then I'll get goin'. You be long, Randall?'

French shook his head. 'Be ready soon as I've done with this excellent breakfast.'

McLain went over to the door, holding the batwings back for Janey to go through. She was wearing a light brown dress with white threading decorating the sleeves and hem. Her hair was piled up behind her head, gleaming golden in the sunlight. McLain thought that she looked very good. She smiled at him and took his arm. He was surprised at the pleasure he felt in the simple gesture.

'You'll be careful?' she asked.

'Sure.' He chuckled. 'You worryin' about me now?'

The girl blushed, not replying. Instead, she began to ask him about the journey. McLain answered her politely, wanting to switch the conversation, but not knowing how. Wanting to tell her she looked pretty and he liked her dress. Wanting to tell her he was pleased at the change in their relationship: frightened to do so.

They reached Donnelly's cabin and went inside. Donnelly was standing looking at the map pinned to the wall. He nodded as they came in.

'Janey. McLain.'

'I'm about ready,' said the Missouri man. 'You want to get Schuyler out?'

Donnelly nodded, something about his manner making McLain feel nervous. The officer took the papers Janey gave him and signed his name with a flourish, then turned to look directly at McLain.

'About last night,' he said. 'I want you to know I'd have stepped in if I'd thought you couldn't handle it.'

McLain was surprised at the admission. It wasn't at all like Frank Donnelly to apologise. Especially not to him. Again he thought that there were definite advantages to being a marshal.

'Forget it,' he said. 'If I couldn't handle it, I wouldn't be doin' this job.'

Janey looked from one man to the other, sensing the difficulty they both had in the exchange. Like two young bulls, she thought, sizing one another up, almost ready to fight. And then another thought came to her as she caught Donnelly's eye: maybe they saw her as the prize. She blushed and said:

'Now the paperwork's done, perhaps we should see John off.'

'Yes.' Donnelly nodded, looking almost grateful for her intervention. 'I just wanted him to know.'

They went out of the office and Donnelly shouted for his men to bring the prisoner out.

'He's all yours, McLain. Good luck.'

'Thanks.'

Neither man offered to shake hands or say anything more, but some kind of agreement had been reached. The old animosity remained, but now it was tinged with grudging respect. And – unspoken – there had been established the tacit acceptance of a dividing line between military and civilian affairs in Garrison.

McLain went back to the corral and fetched the bay out. Shawn had put his saddle on the animal and Schuyler's on a roan. Alice was watching from the stoop, calling that she had put provisions in McLain's saddlebags and that he was to ride careful. McLain nodded, smiling at her. Thinking that a while ago, she'd have put her arms around him and planted a kiss on his cheek. Wondering why she didn't now.

Instead – to his surprise – it was Janey who reached up to put her lips against his skin.

'Be careful,' she murmured. 'Come back safe.'

'Yeah.' He swung into the saddle, fiddling with the bridle to cover his confusion. 'I'll do that.'

He walked the bay down Main Street, leading the roan. Not looking back because he didn't want to get any more confused. There was a faint scent on his cheek where she had kissed him. It seemed to linger in his nostrils.

Donnelly had Schuyler out on the parade ground in front of his cabin. The pockmarked man was still shackled, and Donnelly passed McLain the key. Two soldiers pushed him astride the roan and handed the reins to McLain.

Schuyler said, 'It's a long way to San Antone.'

McLain nodded. 'But you'll get there.'

'Maybe,' grunted Schuyler. 'Maybe not.'

McLain grinned and heeled the bay round to join the group waiting for him by the gates.

The French Seven hands formed a protective group around Schuyler, two siding the man and two falling into line behind. Randall French and McLain rode in front. The promise of the dawn was fulfilled now, the day clear and getting steadily warmer. The air had a lush, lazy feel to it and the grass of the valley bottom shone a luxuriant green in the sparkling light. Under other circumstances McLain would have enjoyed the ride: Randall French was good company, and the hospitality he could expect at the ranch was customarily lavish. Now, however, his mind was on other things. There was the problem of getting Schuyler to San Antonio, which could be either tedious or dangerous. There was the problem of handling his new – official – job when he got back. And there was the problem of what to do about Janey Page.

Exactly what he felt for the woman, he wasn't yet sure. Up to now he hadn't thought much about her one way or the other, except to feel irritated by what he had seen as her Eastern niceties, her disapproval of his direct way of handling things. Now he saw her in a new light. Knew, too, that her attitude had changed. He rubbed absently at his cheek, wondering if he could still smell her scent there, or if it was just his imagination. He decided it was best not to think of her at all. At least not until he returned. He concentrated on the road ahead, pushing her from his mind.

Randall French sensed his mood and had the tact to keep quiet. Behind them, Ben Schuyler rode in silence, wrapped in his own thoughts as the French Seven cowboys watched him the way they'd look at a caged wolf.

They reached the invisible borderline marking the French Seven land off from the public domain and turned towards the ranch house. It had gone up while the Civil War was still raging away to the north and east. Unlike McLain, French had taken no amnesty. He had been invalided out of Jubal Early's command with a leg mangled and stiffened by a Minié ball, his allegiance to the bleeding Southland undimmed by his disgust with the carnage. With six like-minded men he had looked for a place to settle. Somewhere he could raise cows to provide the South with much-needed meat. The war had ended, but – on a smaller, though no less bloody scale – the carnage had continued. There had been Comanche raids, easing off as the Army established itself in the valley and a tenuous truce came into being. There had been bandit attacks. Once – in the not too distant past – there had been the makings of a range war. French had been the leader of the seven-man partnership, and now he was the only one left: six markers showed the last resting places of his friends.

He had built well, siting his house on a low knoll that commanded a spread of rich bottomland. It was a big adobe and timber place, roofed with wood and plastered with clay against the danger of fire arrows. He had supervised the construction of a brushwood fence around the knoll, designed as much to break a Nokoni charge as to pen the seed bulls within its confines. Inside the fence, in addition to the house itself, there was a bunkhouse for the hired hands, a scatter of outbuildings, a feed barn and a corral. Behind the house the six grave markers stood in mute testimony to the struggle.

French smiled as he approached the place: a man coming home. A Mexican stepped down from the shade of the verandah to take the reins of his horse. French climbed down stiffly, favouring his damaged leg.

He turned to his men, pointing his hickory cane at Schuyler. 'Lock him up in one of the sheds. See he gets fed.'

McLain wondered if he should add something about them not laying hands on the prisoner, then decided it wasn't worth it: Randall French kept tight discipline. Instead, he followed the limping man into the house.

Inside it was cool and airy; built Mexican style, with a big room dominated by a vast fireplace taking up most of the ground floor, a wide staircase leading up to a balcony with rooms opening off. French went over to a glass-fronted cabinet and produced a crystal decanter and two glasses.

'Lay the dust, John?'

'Thanks.' McLain took the brandy, savouring the rich, expensive taste.

'Guess you'll be glad to get this done,' French remarked. 'Not a pleasant duty.'

'It ain't much fun,' McLain nodded.

'Still, it shouldn't happen again.' French set the decanter on the big oak table at the centre of the room and eased into a chair. 'With the proper authorisation, you can handle things like this yourselves. Could have this time, really.'

'How so?' McLain frowned. 'Whole point was to make it legal.'

'Of course.' French smiled. 'But there's not a judge in the territory would bat an eye if you'd hung Schuyler back in Garrison. That wasn't the point at all. The point was – is – to get Garrison recognised as a bona fide town. To establish its right to have a marshal and hold trials itself. Without reference to outsiders.'

'I guess.' McLain smiled cynically. 'So we hang a man to bring law in.'

'Yes.' French nodded. 'Something like that. A means to an end.'

McLain went on smiling, no humour showing on his face.

'I never figured on anything like that when I said I'd do it, Randall. That way of thinking's kinda sick.'

'Not sick.' French shook his head. 'Complicated, perhaps, but the law is complicated. Unless you follow it to the letter you don't have any.'

'Was simpler before,' murmured McLain.

'But now civilization is coming,' answered French. 'The way I see things, there'll be settlers swarming into this territory over the next few years. Unless you establish the rule of law early, you'll multiply your problems later. This way no one can argue that Garrison doesn't have law. No one can say the marshal doesn't follow the law.'

He stood up, leaning on his cane.

'I'm going to soak this damn' leg in a hot tub. Make yourself at home.'

McLain nodded, reaching for the decanter. French was an educated man, so he probably knew what he was talking about. The trouble was, McLain didn't follow all the convolutions of the argument.

They ate well that evening, French providing succulent steaks of his prime beef, with vegetables from the patch his Mexican cook tended out back of the house. The meal was washed down with red wine the rancher had shipped in from Galveston, and McLain went up to his room feeling pleasantly relaxed by the liquor.

He awoke while the sun was still fighting its way through the opalescent grey of the dawn, taking advantage of the big bathtub before going down to breakfast. When he was finished eating, he said his goodbyes and collected Schuyler from the outbuilding. The man was subdued, saying nothing as McLain got him mounted and lashed his ankles to the stirrups.

It was another clear day, hotter than before, with no cloud showing in the great sweep of blue sky, unbroken save for the wheeling specks of gulls flown in from the distant coast. McLain put a rope on the roan's bridle, looping it to his own saddlehorn, then heeled the bay to an easy canter. It was close on a week's ride to San Antonio and the country was open all the way. There was some danger of running into Comanches, but he hoped the beef French allowed the tribesmen to run off would reduce the danger of hostile activity. The Mexican bandits who had once regarded the valley as a fair target for raids were mostly fended off by the Army, and there had been no word of outlaw activity in some time. He hoped for a quiet ride.

And got it all the way to Mexican Tom's place.

The way station had been deserted ever since the half-breed Mexican and his Yaqui wife were killed by Zac Moffat's gunmen, falling steadily into a worse state of disrepair than even Tom had allowed. But it still offered the only fresh water in a long way, and McLain planned to spend a night there.

Caution prompted him to rein in and survey the solitary building before going closer. He was surprised to see smoke lifting from the chimney and horses in the corral. Schuyler came up alongside as he watched, pockmarked face splitting in an ugly grin.

'Gettin' nervous, feller?'

'Just cautious.' McLain took the horses forwards at a walk. 'Won't make no difference to you.'

A man came out on to the stoop as he approached. He was a curious figure, hair a grey cut through with streaks of fading black, a ruffled shirt fastened at the neck with a voluminous tie. He wore no gun and raised a hand in greeting.

'Well met, my friends! Veritable Samaritans on this lonely road.'

'Christ!' Schuyler grunted. 'What's he talkin' about?'

McLain grinned, recognising Winston DeVere.

From inside the shack a woman's voice called, 'Who you talking to, Winny?'

'Fellow travellers, my dear.' DeVere went on smiling as he explained, 'My wife. Mrs Ramona DeVere.'

McLain dismounted. 'Thought you'd be long gone. What happened?'

'The rigours of the open road.' The actor's baritone voice took on a tragic note. 'One of the pitfalls that await such as we. The ill-luck that dogs man's footsteps as he seeks to ply his trade.'

'For Chrissakes!' The woman's voice cut through the oratory. 'Our goddam axle got bust.'

DeVere shrugged, his face mournful. 'My dear lady wife has a direct turn of speech on occasion.'

'I'll take a look,' McLain stooped to loosen Schuyler's bonds and help the man down. 'Soon as I got him fixed up.'

'A prisoner!' DeVere's eyes opened in surprise. 'Fettered, too. What heinous crime is he guilty of?'

'Rape,' said McLain. 'An' murder.'

'I ain't having no goddam rapist in here.' Ramona DeVere looked up from the stove. Without the make-up she had worn on stage middle-age showed on her narrow face. 'Put him outside with the horses.'

'Sooner keep him where I can see him, ma'am.' McLain pushed Schuyler into a chair and tied his legs. 'He ain't about to harm no one.'

'You a lawman?' The woman wiped a strand of stringy brown hair from her face. 'I don't see no badge.'

'He's on his way to get it,' said Schuyler. 'I'm the price.'

'Blood shall beget blood,' intoned DeVere. 'Those who live by the sword shall . . .'

'Shut up!' snapped the woman, still looking at McLain. 'Well?'

'It ain't official yet,' he said, wondering why he was bothering to explain. 'I got elected by the folks back in Garrison.'

'Aha! The trouble that so disrupted our performance.' DeVere gestured dramatically at Schuyler. 'This is the man responsible?'

'Yeah.' McLain nodded. 'That's him.'

'He deserves all calumny,' announced the actor. 'Let justice take its course.'

It was hard to tell whether he referred to the crime or to the disruption of his performance. McLain let him ramble on, going out the door to circle round to the corral.

The wagon was there, painted sides bright in the setting sun. It was canted over at an angle, the left-side rear wheel jutting out. McLain got down on his knees, peering below the bed. The axle was snapped about three-quarters the way down its length, the break clean.

He stood up, dusting his pants. And a face came out from between the canvas flaps. A pretty face, capped by a mop of auburn curls. The full mouth was smiling, the green eyes mischievous.

'Well, hello.' Her voice was soft, lilting. 'I'm Decima DeVere. You can call me Deci.'

She stepped clear of the wagon, reaching out so that McLain moved automatically to help her. She was wearing a green dress, cut low at the front. As she moved into his arms, McLain was aware that she wore nothing under the dress. She went on smiling at him, pressing against him longer than was necessary.

'My, you're a big man,' she murmured. 'What's your name?'

'McLain,' he said, freeing himself. 'John T. McLain.'

Decima DeVere repeated the name. 'I like that. John T. McLain. It suits you.'

McLain grunted. From inside the shack, Ramona called, 'Deci? Get yourself in here right now.'

The girl pouted. 'I thought I'd take a walk, momma. I thought John T. McLain might like to accompany me.'

'Right now!' called the woman. 'You leave that man alone.'

The girl stamped her foot, swinging round so that her dress swirled, exposing a length of trim ankle. She glanced back at McLain.

'You'll be staying the night?'

The way she said it, it sounded like she was inviting him into a mansion. Inviting him to a lot more. He nodded, 'Yeah.' And watched her hips sway as she went round the side of the way station.

He went over to the tack shed, hoping the gear Mexican Tom had kept there was intact. The half-breed had lived in hopes of the stage line resuming business, and so kept a quantity of tools and spare parts in readiness. The shed was beginning to fall in on itself, and when he opened the door a spill of dust cascaded from the roof. Thick cobwebs hung from the walls, strung between the bits of harness suspended from rusting nails. Wheels were stacked in one corner, a pile of rat-eaten grain sacks in another. Over against the far wall there was a jumbled pile of tools and other pieces of equipment. McLain batted cobwebs out of his way and began to rummage amongst the stuff. He found an axle that was in good repair and dragged it out. It was about the right size and he thought he could get it fitted on the DeVere wagon. He dropped it by the vehicle and went back inside the shack.

Decima DeVere was helping her mother dole food on to tin plates. Winston was sitting on an upturned barrel, pouring whiskey from a silver hipflask. Ben Schuyler was slumped in his chair, his eyes fastened on the cleavage of the girl's dress.

'A drink, my friend?' DeVere offered the hipflask to McLain. 'A libation to our rescuer.'

'Can you get it fixed?' asked Ramona.

McLain nodded. 'With help, ma'am. We'll do it come daylight.'

He took the flask from DeVere's hand and drank the whiskey. Schuyler took his gaze off the girl just long enough to watch him drink. He licked his lips and went back to studying Decima. There was an ugly sparkle in his dark eyes.

After they had eaten, the two women made up beds over to one side of the shack. McLain stretched Schuyler on the floor, fastening the shackles around an upright. He stretched himself on the planks, head resting on his saddle.

Schuyler murmured, 'Ain't she somethin'? Don't that get yore juices flowin', McLain?'

The big man grunted, 'Shut yore mouth.'

From the darkness across the room Decima DeVere laughed softly.

Chapter Eleven

McLain washed at the pump, then set to greasing the axle. By the time he was finished the DeVere women were up, and Winston came out. McLain noticed that the grey was gone from his hair, replaced by glossy black. The actor caught his look and shrugged, vaguely embarrassed.

'A slight subterfuge, my dear friend. One's audience somehow respects one more whilst the countenance of youth remains.'

As best McLain could tell, he was saying he dyed his hair.

'We'll need to block her up.' He pointed at the wagon. 'Then I can take the wheels off an' get the new axle fitted in.'

'Ah, yes.' DeVere nodded solemnly. 'I shall help all I can, needless to say. But physical exertion has never been my strong point.'

McLain shrugged and went inside the shack. He got Schuyler free of the upright and fastened the shackles back on the man's wrists.

'You're gonna need me to help lift that, ain't you?' the man demanded. 'Hafta take these off.'

'When I need you,' McLain said evenly. 'Not before. Don't try anythin'.'

Schuyler grinned and began to scoop eggs off his plate. Ramona DeVere set a coffee pot down and Decima brought a plate of hot biscuits over. She smiled at McLain.

Schuyler said, 'Ain't no use makin' eyes at him, little lady. He's got hisself a woman back in Garrison.'

McLain glowered at him, not saying anything.

'Is that right?' Decima asked, pouting theatrically. 'Is she pretty?'

'No,' said McLain. 'Yes.'

The girl laughed. 'Why, John T. McLain. I do believe you're tongue-tied.'

'And you've got a loose one,' snapped her mother. 'You mind it, missy. Don't go prying into other folk's business.'

McLain was glad of the intervention. The directness of the question had taken him by surprise and he felt the confusion he had pushed from his mind coming back. To hide his awkwardness he rose to his feet.

'Let's go.'

'I ain't done eatin',' Schuyler complained.

'They'll give you a hearty breakfast in San Antone.' McLain grabbed the man's collar and hauled him to his feet. 'Right now we got work to do.'

He took Schuyler outside and set him to piling adobe to make a pivot for the pole they'd need to lift the wagon. When it was ready, he fetched a solid-looking length of timber from the shack and got it in place, one end thrust under the wagon, the centre balanced on the piled bricks. DeVere came over, looking dubious. Decima came out to watch.

'You got a gun?' McLain asked DeVere.

The actor nodded, producing a Deringer. McLain took it and handed it to the girl.

'You know how to use that?'

She nodded.

'Good.' McLain took the shackles off Schuyler's wrists. 'He tries anything, you shoot him.'

Decima licked her lips, staring nervously at the pock-marked man. Schuyler grinned at her and said, 'Ain't the kind of bang you like, is it?'

The girl blushed and levelled the little pistol in both hands. McLain shoved the man into position, then showed DeVere where he should take the pole. McLain fetched loose adobe over and piled it up under the wagon, almost touching the bed. Then he joined the others and began to heave.

The wagon rose slowly, the pole straining under the

weight. McLain called for Schuyler and DeVere to keep it in position and moved round to stack more adobe under the bed. It was dangerous leaving Schuyler loose on the pole, but he didn't trust either man to stack the blocks right. He went back and lent his own weight to their efforts. The wagon rose some more, and he added more adobe to the mounting pile. A few more inches, he reckoned, and the vehicle would be lifted high enough he could work the broken axle loose. He joined the others and called for a fresh effort. The wagon creaked higher still. McLain let go the pole and stooped down to finish stacking the blocks.

Then DeVere shouted and he snatched his hands away a fraction of a second before they got crushed under the falling wagon bed. He ducked, twisting round. Not quite fast enough to avoid the edge of the thing slamming against his shoulder. Knocking him flat. Numbing his right arm.

Decima screamed.

Adobe dust blinded McLain.

He rolled on his back, coming up on his feet with his right arm hanging loose by his side, blinking the dust from his eyes.

'Hold it right there!' Schuyler's voice was harsh. 'You move, an' the girl gets it.'

He was standing with his left arm around Decima DeVere, pinning her hands to her sides. His hand was clutched tight over her right breast, fingers digging through the material of her green dress. The Deringer was in his right hand, muzzle pressed against the girl's temple.

McLain realised that he was beyond the sure range of accuracy of the little hideaway. It didn't do him much good, except maybe to save his life: his own gun hand was too numb to draw. And he couldn't chance it, anyway. Not with the Deringer cocked against the girl's skull.

'Drop yore belt,' snarled Schuyler.

McLain made a fast decision. The Deringer was a single-shot: if the pockmarked man used it on Decima, he'd have nothing to stop McLain killing him. No more bullets. No more shield.

McLain shook his head.

'I'll blow her goddam skull off,' grated Schuyler.

'No, you won't.' McLain used the same tone he'd employed facing Hansen's lynch mob. 'You only got the one shot before I kill you.'

Schuyler grinned nastily. 'All right. It's a stand-off, then. Only this time you don't have no Comanches to help you out. You ain't gonna stop me ridin' out.'

'I'll come after you,' rasped McLain. 'You know that.'

'I'm takin' the girl,' Schuyler grated. 'You ain't gonna try anything so long as I got her.'

Decima began to weep, her face getting ugly as the full danger of her situation registered.

'Saddle that bay.' Schuyler spoke to DeVere. 'Turn the others loose. Then bring the bay over here.'

DeVere hurried to obey. His wife came out from the shack and screamed as she saw her daughter's predicament.

Schuyler yelled, 'Shut yore goddam mouth.'

She shut it, pressing both hands to her lips as though stifling the sound of her own screaming. Her eyes were huge and frightened as she watched her husband lead the saddled bay over.

'Here.' All the pompous oratory was gone from the actor's voice. 'Your horse.'

Schuyler backed towards the animal, still holding Decima between himself and McLain. He swung into the saddle too fast for the big Missouri man to cross the distance, and leant over to press the Deringer against the girl's hair as he dragged her face down across the saddle. McLain caught a brief glimpse of her features before her hair came unpinned and fell down in a tumble of red. They were distorted by terror.

'You try followin' me an' I'll kill her.' Schuyler walked the bay past McLain. 'You remember that.'

'I'll remember.' McLain's voice was harsh.

Schuyler chuckled and drove his heels hard against the gelding's flanks, sending the animal forwards in a gallop that blew dust into McLain's face. The big man watched him go, rubbing at his shoulder. It was too numb yet to chance a shot at a moving target. And Schuyler still had the Deringer pressed against the girl's head.

'Don't just stand there!' Ramona DeVere's voice was shrill. 'Go after the bastard!'

'He'll kill her,' warned her husband. 'You heard what he said.'

'Not yet.' McLain fetched his rope out, looking to where the other horses were grazing the prairie. 'Not Schuyler.'

'What do you mean?' asked DeVere.

'I told you why I was takin' him in,' grated McLain. 'There's something comes before the killing.'

'Oh, my God!' Ramona DeVere began to weep.

Chapter Twelve

McLain got his rope on the roan horse and mounted bareback, herding the wagon team back inside the corral. The DeVeres watched in nervous silence as he saddled up, thankful that Schuyler had been in too much of a hurry to remember the Sharps or the second Dragoon stowed in his saddlebags. He handed the big pistol to Winston.

Ramona said, 'You'll bring her back, won't you?'

'If I can.' He looked at her tear-stained face. 'I'll do my best.'

Before she could say anything more he turned the horse eastwards and took off after Schuyler. The way he had it figured, the pockmarked man would make a run for San Antonio in hopes of losing himself in the city. With only the Deringer he wasn't likely to risk turning north into Comanche country, and back to the west he'd be heading into Garrison again; southwards, there was just a lot of open country stretching down to the Mexican border. The girl would slow him, but McLain felt pretty sure he wouldn't dump her until he'd taken his pleasure. It all depended on catching up with him before.

It had taken McLain around an hour to bring the horses in, and Schuyler was on a better mount than the roan. But he had been pushing the gelding at a pace too fast to maintain for long without winding the animal, so in time he'd have to slow down. McLain held the roan to a steady canter, counting on endurance rather than speed to bring him up with his quarry

Decima DeVere felt the saddle thud painfully against her stomach. Spittle from the horse's mouth flecked her face and hair, and gradually physical discomfort overcame her fear. After all, the pockmarked man hadn't killed her, even though her weight must be slowing him down. She wriggled, and felt his hand clamp on her buttocks.

'I'm hurting,' she called.

To her surprise, Schuyler reined in and helped her to the ground. She stood rubbing at the ache where the saddlehorn had dug against her. Then began to wipe her face and rearrange her hair. Schuyler watched her with hooded eyes. It was a look she recognised: familiar after twenty-three years travelling with her parents. That he would kill her if he thought it necessary, she did not doubt. But not yet. There was something he wanted first. And if she could persuade him it was worth having a second time, then she might live a little longer. Maybe long enough to get away, or long enough for John T. McLain to catch up.

She smiled at him; cautiously. And he grinned back. Take away the pockmarks and he wouldn't be a bad-looking man. Better than some she had known. Who had known her.

'You're pretty,' he said. 'Real pretty.'

'Thank you.' Her voice was dry with dust and fear: husky. She hoped it sounded seductive. 'Are you really what McLain said?'

Schuyler went on grinning. 'I been in trouble.'

'A road agent!' She chose deliberately to misunderstand. 'How romantic! I've never met a real road agent before.'

He shrugged, and she sensed a slight shifting of the odds in her favour.

'Where are you taking me?'

'East.' Schuyler looked back down the trail. 'Hafta get away from that bastard McLain.'

'Shouldn't we be riding, then?' Instinct warned her to group them together. Partners. 'Before he catches us?'

'Horse needs rest,' he grunted. 'Besides, it'll take him a spell to round the others up.'

'You know best.' She began to straighten her dress, bending forwards to emphasise her cleavage.

'Yeah.' Schuyler nodded. 'Let's walk.'

She fell into step beside him, staying close enough that every so often her hip brushed against him. She kept a smile fixed on her face, thinking that she had to keep him interested, had to persuade him it was better to keep her alive.

'You can handle him,' she murmured. 'You did before.'

'He's got guns.' Schuyler spat into the dust. 'I shoulda thought of that. All I got's this lousy Deringer.'

'Can't you get more?' she asked, with what she hoped was the right degree of confidence in him. 'I'm sure *you* can.'

'Ain't nowhere to get them. Ain't nothin' between us an' San Antone.'

'Is that where you're taking me?' She looked at him through a strand of hair; coquettish. 'They have big hotels there. With soft beds.'

Schuyler glanced at her, his face puzzled.

'Maybe.'

She swallowed hard and fell silent. Don't overdo it, she told herself. Play it careful. Don't push it.

After a while Schuyler announced that they could ride again. He climbed into the saddle and reached a hand down to her. She took it and let him lift her up in front. She said nothing as he put an arm around her, cupping a breast in his right hand. Instead, she leant back against him, letting her hair touch his face, shifting slightly so that her breast pressed harder against his grip. It might have been hysteria that made her smile as she realised her nipples were hardening.

McLain followed the road eastwards. It cut straight across the grasslands, a greyish ribbon of hard-packed dirt that was rutted with wagon tracks. Either side, the grass grew thick and rich, dense enough to show clearly any deviation from the trail. Schuyler must have spotted that and decided to push straight on. Ahead, the country got broken up into folds, cut through with gulleys and thickets of mesquite. Schuyler could turn off there, confident of leaving no clear trail to follow.

McLain lifted the roan to a faster pace, glancing up at the sun.

It was a little after noon, the golden disc shifted slightly over to the west. The sky was a translucent blue, streaked with mares' tails of white high up where the wind off the coast hit. There was no sign of Schuyler or the girl on the road ahead, and McLain guessed they would reach the broken country before he caught up.

He went on riding.

Dogged. Determined.

Not thinking about anything except gaining on the pockmarked man and bringing him back.

The sun shifted further across the sky. McLain's shadow lengthened in front of him. Cattle watched him pass, bovine eyes staring placidly. He held his pace late into the afternoon, walking the roan horse when it showed signs of tiring, then lifting it back to the steady, mile-eating canter. The sky ahead began to grow dark. Behind him it was a furnace red, streaked with burnished gold along the rimrock of the distant Eagle Range. The air grew still with that quietude that precedes the abrupt descent of night. The moon showed against the darkening velvet, a thin, rising sliver. McLain slowed to little more than a walk, wary of injuring the horse on the increasingly broken ground.

'Are we stopping?'

The girl turned her head as she spoke, brushing her cheek against Schuyler's, letting her body shiver slightly as the air got cooler.

'Soon.' Schuyler's voice was hoarse. His hand tightened on her breast so that she needed to grit her teeth to stop herself from wincing. 'Not long.'

He steered the bay gelding along the bed of a dry wash, turning off through a patch of mesquite and cholla. For the last hour, as dusk turned into full night and the moon replaced the sun, he had been winding a circuitous course through the broken terrain. Decima guessed that he was hiding his tracks, seeking to use what remained of the light to find some safe place to spend the night.

She trembled as she realised that before long he would reach a decision. That soon she would need all her natural wiles and all the dramatic guile taught her by her parents to ensure her safety.

'What's wrong?' Schuyler felt her trembling. 'You frightened of me?'

'I'm cold,' she said, hoping it was the right thing: there were some men who liked to think they scared women. And God knew, Schuyler scared her. 'I'm frightened, too. I've never been kidnapped by a road agent.'

Schuyler chuckled. There was something anticipatory in the sound. He turned the horse around a knoll commanding a view of the surrounding terrain and halted.

'This'll do.'

He helped her down, hands running over her hips, staring at her face with his tongue flicking over his lips. He took the saddle off the bay and tethered the animal. Then led the way to the crest of the knoll. The hummock was thick with bushes that grew in a circle around the bare top. It was sandy, still warm from the day's sun.

'We got nothin' to eat,' he grunted. 'An' we can't risk no fire.'

She noticed that he said *we*, not *I*. And smiled: 'I can keep you warm.'

He stared at her, his face curious. 'Ain't you scared?'

'I was thinking.' She said it quickly, conscious of playing the most important role of her life. 'When we get to San Antonio, McLain will be looking for a man on his own. Not a couple. Not a man and woman together.'

'Yeah.' Schuyler went on frowning. 'You got a point.'

She felt the night wind flatten her dress against her body. It was a sensual feeling, like caressing fingers stroking her flesh. She realised that the odds were shifting further in her favour. That she was even beginning to enjoy this role she was playing.

'Ladies love outlaws,' she murmured. 'Didn't you know that?'

Schuyler shook his head. 'I never met a lady.'

'Before.' She admonished softly.

And reached for the fastenings of her dress.

It came away in a soft murmur of cloth. The cooling air – or perhaps excitement – made her nipples stand out hard from the smooth mounds of her breasts. Moonlight shone silvery on the dark triangle between her thighs. She knew she had a good body. Schuyler wasn't the first man to see it: she hoped he wouldn't be the last.

'I don't know your first name,' she whispered.

'Ben,' he said; throatily.

'Take off your clothes, Ben.'

Schuyler swallowed hard, hands tugging at buttons. At his belt.

He stood naked, facing her. She noticed that he had placed the Deringer under his saddle. She stepped close to him, hands twining about his neck, ignoring the sour odour of sweat, feeling excitement rise in her own body as she felt him stiffen against her. She pressed closer, using her tongue and her breasts and her hips to arouse him more. Using every trick she knew to concentrate his attention on the one thing.

She slid to the ground, drawing him down with her, pushing him on to his back as she rolled astride him. She felt suddenly powerful. Felt, as she moved against him, that she was in control now. She moaned, using her body. Using his lust.

McLain dismounted.

It was full dark now and the moon wasn't bright enough to allow for sure tracking. He knew that Schuyler had turned off the trail and guessed the pockmarked man was looking for someplace to hole up for the night. He put himself in Schuyler's situation: the bay would need resting after carrying the double load, and the runaway had to know McLain was coming after him. That would most likely mean he'd look for a place he could use defensively. Somewhere he could watch the surrounding ground. Somewhere high.

There was the jut of a knoll sticking up black a little way off. Even if Schuyler wasn't there, it would give McLain some advantage come daylight. He moved towards it, leading the roan. Slow. Cautious.

He halted in the deep shadow of the wash and left the horse tethered, his bandanna wound around the nostrils, as he moved forwards on foot. He climbed the bank and circled the knoll. Then grinned tightly as he saw the bay horse foraging in the mesquite.

Warily, silently, he clambered up the knoll.

And halted, gaping in surprise as he reached the crest.

Ben Schuyler was on his back. His head was resting against his saddle and his arms were up around Decima DeVere's waist, hands stroking the girl's hips and buttocks as she moved rhythmically against him. Schuyler was moaning softly, thrusting against the girl with eyes and mouth wide open.

McLain had expected rape, but not like this.

He drew the big Dragoon and came through the bushes at a run.

Decima screamed.

Schuyler yelled something McLain couldn't make out and jerked his body up, hurling the girl clear. She landed on her side, still screaming as she rolled over and struggled upright directly in McLain's path.

He ran into her, tripping on her flailing limbs so that he lurched forwards, off balance. She clutched at him and he cursed her, shoving clear as the pockmarked man twisted to get his right hand under the saddle.

The Deringer came out, muzzle pointed at McLain's face. He saw the hammer go back. Schuyler's knuckle whiten as he squeezed the trigger. He flattened against the sand, blinded by muzzle flash, feeling the slug whip his hat from his head close enough his hair was ruffled by its passage.

And then Schuyler was on him. His hands fastened on McLain's wrist, twisting the Dragoon away. Pounding the gun against the ground. McLain felt his fingers numb and spring open, letting go of the Dragoon. Schuyler reached for it, and McLain brought his left hand up and round, slamming his fist into the pockmarked man's side. Schuyler grunted and fell sideways.

McLain pivoted on his hip, swinging both legs over to drive his feet against Schuyler's ribs, rolling him over away from the pistol. The outlaw snarled and came upright. He looked primeval, a naked savage, his face contorted with rage and hatred. McLain dived for the gun. And Schuyler came down on top of him with hands like claws fastening on his throat. Yanking his head back, cutting off his breath. McLain forgot about the pistol and reached up to grab Schuyler's wrists. He forced them apart, sucking in a choking lungful of oxygen. Schuyler got his knees in the small of McLain's back and began to pull against the Missouri man's grip.

McLain let go of his wrists and felt fists slam against his skull. He fought over on to his back, twisting his head aside as Schuyler landed a punch. He got his knees bent and pushed hard, throwing the man off. Schuyler rolled, coming upright again with an agility born of fear and hate and fury. He kicked McLain in the face. Again in the belly. McLain grunted and lurched back, tottering to his feet as Schuyler came in with his features distorted in a feral snarl. McLain sidestepped a windmilling punch and drove a fist into the man's belly. Another against his head. Schuyler staggered.

McLain swung a third punch that landed on the side of his jaw, snapping his mouth wide open, his head to the side.

Schuyler screamed like a panther and sprang directly at McLain. His legs wound around the big man's, his arms pinning McLain's. His head butted, slamming against McLain's nose and teeth. They went down again, rolling over and over as the girl went on screaming and McLain fought to free his hands.

He got one loose and grabbed a fistful of hair, forcing Schuyler's butting head away. The outlaw transferred his grip to McLain's throat, fingers digging against the windpipe. McLain punched him in the neck, and Schuyler gagged. McLain hit him again. On the mouth. The side of the head. Schuyler bared his teeth and tried to bite McLain's throat. Panic lent him strength and McLain felt his teeth snap together, scoring a patch of skin ragged. He put a hand over Schuyler's face and began to push. The man was like an animal now, not trying to punch, but clawing and biting in blind fury. McLain slammed a bunched fist against his jaw. Once. A second time. A third.

Schuyler's legs loosened and McLain wriggled clear. He came up on his feet as the outlaw launched himself through the air. McLain sidestepped, kicking high and hard. The toe of his boot caught Schuyler in the groin, doubling him over as a high-pitched scream burst from his open mouth. He landed heavily and McLain stepped forwards, kicking out again to drive his boot against Schuyler's chin. The gaping mouth snapped shut. Teeth splintered. McLain went down on his knees, right arm raised above his head. He brought it down in a savage swing that drove the point of his elbow against Schuyler's midriff. The outlaw grunted, frothing at the mouth. McLain hit his head, feeling the nose pulp under his fist.

Schuyler gasped and went limp.

McLain climbed to his feet, panting. He picked up the Dragoon. The Deringer. Decima DeVere stared at him with huge eyes. She was breathing hard and one hand was touching between her legs. McLain picked up her dress and tossed it to her. The girl gasped in surprise.

'Get dressed.' His voice was angry. He wasn't sure why. 'Cover yoreself.'

She tugged the dress on, still breathing hard.

'It's not worse than death,' she said; defiantly.

'No,' grunted McLain. 'I guess not.'

He went over to where Schuyler lay groaning and rolled the man on to his back.

'It's all over,' he said. 'It's finished now.'

Schuyler spat blood and pieces of broken tooth. The fight was gone out of him now and his nakedness looked only pathetic. McLain threw him his clothes, holding the Dragoon levelled from the waist.

When Schuyler was dressed, McLain prodded him down the slope to the bay horse. At gunpoint, he made the outlaw saddle the animal, then told Decima to mount. With Schuyler out in front, he walked down to where he had left the roan. He put Schuyler in the saddle and tied his wrists to the horn; his ankles to the stirrups. Then he climbed up in front of the girl and headed back in the direction of the way station.

'A veritable knight errant!' Winston DeVere threw his arms wide as though to embrace McLain. 'What good fortune sent you our way, my dear friend! What propitious god smiled upon us when he directed your footsteps to our humble resting place!'

'What happened?' Ramona DeVere looked at her daughter, then at McLain. 'Did he . . . ?'

'No.' McLain shook his head. 'He didn't rape her.'

It wasn't a lie, and neither the girl nor Schuyler saw fit to explain just what had happened. Decima threw the big Missouri man a grateful look and climbed into the wagon.

When she emerged again, she was wearing a blue dress

and her hair was pinned back in place. She looked almost demure.

'We'll get the wagon fixed,' McLain announced. 'I'll ride with you to San Antone.'

This time, he left Schuyler's wrists shackled as they lifted the vehicle and he clambered underneath to shift the broken axle. Ramona held the Deringer. She kept it cocked and pressed up against the outlaw's ribs. Schuyler didn't try anything.

McLain got the replacement axle in position and fitted the wheels back on the hubs. He put Schuyler inside, tying him securely. As he mounted the bay, Decima came up to him and touched his arm.

'Thank you,' she murmured. 'For everything.'

McLain grinned at her, the anger he had felt back on the knoll forgotten.

'Just doin' my duty, ma'am. Keepin' the peace.'

She nodded and climbed on to the seat alongside her parents. Winston flipped the reins and the wagon rumbled out on to the trail. McLain rode out in front, still smiling as he felt the sun warm on his face. Whatever else he might think about Decima DeVere, he had to admit she was one hell of a good actress.

San Antonio rose out of the flatlands like a promise. The buildings stood tall and white and welcoming, the Spanish influence showing in their construction, elegant and cool-looking after the heat of the trail. McLain left the DeVeres at a cheap hotel in the downtown section, accepting Winston's handshake and effusive promises to return to Garrison. Ramona hugged him and thanked him in more ordinary language. Decima kissed him full on the mouth.

'If we do come back,' she said, 'I'd like to thank you properly.'

McLain smiled and wondered if that was a good idea: there was something about the girl that spelled trouble in capital letters. He turned away, walking down the street with the two horses behind him, Ben Schuyler slumped resignedly in the saddle.

He found the sheriff's office and took the outlaw inside.

A tall man with the beginnings of a gut looked up from behind a desk littered with wanted posters. A nameplate on the desk said he was Sheriff Wilf Stodard.

'Got a prisoner for you.' McLain shoved Schuyler forwards. 'Got a report, too.'

Stodard locked Schuyler in a cell and read the papers Janey Page had prepared. He frowned, tugging at the luxuriant moustache covering his upper lip and most of his mouth.

'I never seen anythin' like this before,' he said. 'I best take you to see Judge Lefevre.'

They went out of the office and walked down to a two-storey building fronted by a large square of neatly-trimmed grass. There was a gallows at the centre of the square. Its woodwork was polished, gleaming in the sun. The machinery of the trap-door was oiled, efficient-looking. Stodard went past it without a glance. He led the way inside the building and knocked on a big, highly-polished door.

From inside, a voice called: 'Enter.'

'Judge.' Stodard removed his hat. 'Got the damndest thing here. Take a look.'

Lefevre was a short, fat man. His hair was grey and slicked down with pomade. He wore a black suit with a fancy waistcoat spanned by a heavy gold watch chain. He produced a pair of pince-nez spectacles to read Janey's report, and as he read his florid face got redder. Finally he began to chuckle. McLain began to feel awkward.

'So you want to be a marshal?' Lefevre asked.

'It's what folks in Garrison want,' McLain replied. 'We figger we need proper law.'

The judge's cheeks wobbled. 'And you want this man Ben Schuyler hung?'

'Legal,' said McLain. 'Done proper.'

'Very well.' Lefevre nodded. 'That all?'

'Ain't that enough?' McLain wondered what was so damn' funny.

'You could have done it there,' said the judge. 'All you needed do was get a Citizens' Committee together. They could've made you marshal legal as me. Hung Schuyler the same way.'

McLain didn't know whether he felt like laughing or losing his temper. He stared at Lefevre and at Stodard, not saying anything.

'All right.' Lefevre took a Bible and a badge from his desk. 'Raise your right hand and repeat after me . . .'

The ceremony took little more than a minute. McLain repeated the words of the oath with his hand on the Bible. Lefevre came around the desk and pinned the badge on his shirt.

'Now you're a duly appointed officer of the law,' he said. 'I'll deal with Schuyler tomorrow.'

It was a bright May day. There was only a small crowd gathered as Stodard and McLain took Schuyler up the steps of the gallows. Judge Lefevre was watching from the balcony of the courthouse and the hangman looked like he was in a hurry to get it done. Schuyler's pockmarked face was impassive: like a man who knows he's come to the end of the line and is resigned to his fate. The hangman asked if he had any last words.

'Yeah.' Schuyler looked at McLain and grinned. 'Thanks for givin' me the girl. At least I go out with a bang.'

The hangman put the noose around his neck. Ben Schuyler looked at the sun for one last time. Then the trap swung open and he fell through. His neck broke with an audible crack.

The sun shone bright on McLain's new badge.

Westerns from Fontana

The very best of the West! Hard-hitting stories by some of the world's best Western writers.

William S. Brady
THE SUDDEN GUNS (HAWK 1) 85p
BLOOD MONEY (HAWK 2) 85p
DEATH'S BOUNTY (HAWK 3) 85p
KILLING TIME (HAWK 4) 85p
FOOL'S GOLD (HAWK 5) 85p
BLOOD KIN (HAWK 6) 80p
THE GATES OF DEATH (HAWK 7) 85p

Frank C. Robertson
THE VALLEY OF FRIGHTENED MEN 70p

Lewis Patten
GUNS AT GREY BUTTE 70p
THE RUTHLESS RANGE 70p

W. C. Tuttle
WOLF CREEK VALLEY 65p

Clifton Adams
DOOMSDAY CREEK 65p

and many others

Fontana Paperbacks